Also by J. Wilder-Hall

Poetry

The History of the World

What Could We Have Possibly Known About Love Then?

Love Poems and Other Stories
An American Debut
Vol. 2

J. Wilder-Hall

All rights reserved. For information, address Thompson Woods Publishing, PO Box 676, Fairfield, CT 06824.

Printed in the United States of America

ISBN 978-1-7342383-3-4 (pbk.)

Book jacket and design by L.R. Pilotti

For my parents

CONTENTS

Her Recommending Hitchens (from the Maryann Notebooks)

What Could We Have Possibly Known About Love Then?

We create a language out of what is not so easily understood to get at the heart, and what we believe may lie on the other side of that. Like the ancient Greeks who created a world out of an impossible scale of themselves. What he remembers now remarkably well are the voices of the old-time radio announcers late at night in the middle of a warm summer when he was lying in bed and the skinny brown eyed girl from the record shop he hadn't noticed at first (but with whom he would fall hopelessly in love over the years) had first moved next door and he was not even thirteen years old. Certainly, it is not the five-thousand-mile trip he took with his parents and sister to Spain (as a gift for his high school graduation, his mother gushed, from the preparatory school on Great Barrington Road) and then off to the Sagrada Familia! that seems important anymore. But what has happened to them all those years since that stops him cold in the middle of a life. What is important is what makes us feel alive, what frightens us into a larger awareness of ourselves and deepens our understanding of joy and empathy for others.

Anchors, Wonder Dog and Man's Best Friend
William Doyle Kenney, 1995

From Where We Live to Where We're Going

I'm trying to talk with him about things, *important things,* but he's not listening.

He's reading the paper. He's reading through the list of cars in the auto section.

It says here: Original owner, low mileage, power windows, power steering, *all service records available.* Like new, he says.

He says, Probably some old granny or something, you know?

He takes his pen and circles the ad in the paper. He goes on reading.

He's been doing this for days now!

All of a sudden he's gotten it into his mind that we need a new car, and we need it *pronto,* like yesterday in fact. Like he was the one who was caught on the highway in the driving wind and rain when the alternator went and I was calling and calling practically everyone I knew.

Where the hell was everyone?

A few days after he brought me home *those* flowers is when he announced it. I was on the phone with my sister talking through things—Not that I told her everything. What could I tell her? How much explaining did I have to do?—when suddenly he slams open the door and says: No wife of his is

3

going to be driving that heap of shit car, not on his watch anyways.

Things are going to change around here, he says, and it's about time. If he has to work two, three, four jobs even, he'll do it. He doesn't care. Whatever it takes is what he's willing to do.

Why wouldn't he?

I swear, the last time I remember him talking like this was after that thing with Rita some years ago. Out of all the women we knew, *Rita* for God's sake! *Rita,* the godmother to our eldest, the maid of honor at our wedding, the woman we'd decided to care for our kids should anything ever happen to us—*that Rita!*

I mean isn't anything sacred anymore? *Anything?*

Of course: What are you talking about? is what he said. You don't know *what* you're talking about. *Rita?* Why would I want Rita when I have you?

...And when I talked to Rita about it, she wasn't any better—

So what gives? I said. What's the hurry? What's all this talk all of a sudden?

I mean the last time I tried talking to him he didn't want to hear anything of it. What was there to talk about anyways? It wasn't like we were *Rockefellers.* It wasn't like we had a whole line of money trees. And what about the economy?

Franny, he said, have you thought about the economy?

When he came home with those flowers the day after the kids and I came back from visiting my brother Paul, he said he

4

had this dream, more like a *nightmare* than a dream. He said one night while we were away he'd woken in a pool of sweat.

Franny, I was drenched, he said. *Drenched!* Franny, you wouldn't even believe—

I was trying to get my bearings. I had my suitcase out. I was trying to put away my things when he came over and put his arms around me.

…The stereo was on, I remember. He played this song. He said, Franny, I missed the hell out of you—more than you could ever imagine.

He slid his hands from my hips. We started dancing.

He said practically his whole life I've been the one constant of everything he'd come to know. He said he wouldn't know what to do with himself should anything ever happen to me. There were the kids, sure. But they'd be off on their own soon. They'd go off to college and so on. They'd come around every once in a while, yes. But then who knows what would happen? They were getting to that age. We were *all* getting to that age.

Franny, he said, I thought it was the real deal!

Later that night is when he told me about taking his life back. It's time we start taking our lives back, Fran, he said. It's time we start putting ourselves first. Don't we have that right? Don't we have a right to be happy?

He said, I'm sorry to be the one to tell you, Franny, but we ain't getting any younger. We're not as young as we used to be.

I said, What the hell are you trying to tell me?

He said, What about *our* lives, Franny?

…Ever since he's been doing sit-ups on our bedroom floor—*crunches* he calls them. In the morning, in the evening.

5

What Could We Have Possibly Known About Love Then?

He says sit-ups are one thing, crunches are another. Who does sit-ups anymore? Sit-ups don't do a lick of good for you. He says, Franny, haven't you read any of the health magazines?

But besides the car ads I can't even remember the last time I'd seen him read anything!

So I said something about it. I said, Who told you this? Where are you getting your information? Who was it?

Who? he said. What do you mean *who?*

You should have seen the look on his face. It goddamn near killed me!

Then he said Mike Kelly told him. Mike Kelly, *that's who.* The same Mike Kelly he works with.

Mike Kelly? I said.

My God, out of all the people to choose!

You should see this Mike he's talking about.

Without looking up, he scratches his face and says, Here's a car for you, listen to this—

He reads on for a time. Then he says, Franny, are you listening to me?

He shakes his head like I've said something, like he's agreeing with something I've just said. Then he takes another spoonful of that oatmeal he's been eating, wipes his mouth with the back of his hand and does that thing with his lips like he's searching for something there.

He slugs down the rest of his coffee and pushes the empty cup to the center of the table, right near those flowers from *Hanson's*—those irises, tulips and so on—wrapped with a bow and that *fancy* Hanson's label.

I can't stand it! I mean *really!* I can't even remember the last time I'd seen that label! I mean if my life depended on it there's no way of telling!

When he came home with those flowers, I thought someone died. *My God,* I said, what's wrong? Did something happen? What happened?

I even said to him, Rick, who died? Who died, Rick?

I was in a state of panic to say the least!

Died? Rick said. What do you mean: *died?* Nobody died. Who died? he said in this voice—like *I'm* crazy or something. Then he gave me these eyes. He shrugged his shoulders and yawned.

He had another long day at work. *Him and Mike,* I suppose. He was having a lot of those lately. They were *busy, busy,* he said. He couldn't believe how *busy* they were all of a sudden.

Can't a guy just show his wife how much he loves her? *Jesus,* he said, is there something wrong with that? What's wrong with that?

He laughed.

Oh, Franny, he said. Come here, Franny.

So we started dancing awhile—
I can't even tell you. But then all of a sudden I could feel my heart beating!

…And then afterward he said he told that guy at Hanson's to forget about any notion he might have had of putting even a single rose in that bouquet there. He said, You know how those guys are—"always rose happy." Tell them you want to put a bouquet together for your wife, do something *special,* and they're ready to back the truck up with roses.

But he said he told that guy straight away. He said, You don't know my wife Fran. She'll go *crazy* if she sees even one rose in that bouquet. My wife Fran has this thing with roses.

Roses makes her crazy! he said.

He keeps on reading, then asks me if I wouldn't mind fixing him another cup. Franny, he says, would you?

I wouldn't be surprised if he spent seventy-five dollars on that goddamn bouquet. Probably even a hundred to tell you the truth! Those flowers from Hanson's aren't cheap!

Watching him chew on that oatmeal, I wouldn't mind picking up that bouquet and heaving it square across the room!

Franny, he says, you've got to listen to this. I think this might be the one—

Outside there's the sound of a car door slammed shut and I push back the curtain above the sink some to see that young nurse who's been coming around to look after Mr. Carlson since the fall he suffered this past January. *Poor* Mr. Carlson!

I watch the young nurse all the way to Mr. Carlson's back door. I watch the way her hips *still* go, the way her dress follows. She can't be more than twenty-two or twenty-three years old.

She could be in high school for God's sake!

So I let the curtain fall back, and Rick mixes the last of the bananas with the last of his oatmeal.

I wonder if he's heard her car pull in. If he has, he hasn't said anything. He doesn't even move his eyes. It's like they're glued to the paper, like he doesn't *dare!*

The last time that nurse was brought up, Rick said how lucky Mr. Carlson was to have a good woman taking care of him, how it wasn't easy to find a good woman these days.

From Where We Live to Where We're Going

A diamond in the rough, he says. Not that anybody around here is looking—

I say to him, Rick, did you hear what I said to you? At least, I think I'm saying it.

I return the mug to the table, right where he'd pushed it, and watch the steam rise. I know at any minute things are going to happen here. I've known him long enough to know that.

It's like I can feel it!

But before I can say anything, he says, I know, I know. I know it's a *long-shot,* Franny. I know what you're *thinking,* but maybe there's a way around this, a logical solution. He says there are things that need to be fixed around here. *A lot of things!* Things he's been planning to do for some time now. He says he has a whole list!

Now I know you're not necessarily the pick-up type, he says. So maybe we can work out an agreement, an *arrangement,* he says. And maybe that arrangement is, if things work out this way, he can take the pick-up and I can take his car. Or we can trade off after a while. I can have the pick-up and he can have the car. And vice versa.

Hell, you might really take to driving a pick-up after all. Think about all the things we can do. *Hell,* he says, stranger things have happened.

He gives me this look and shakes the paper. He puts the paper down and reaches for the coffee mug. He does that thing with his lips and his tongue. He starts looking me over. He starts looking at my legs and thighs, he starts looking at my breasts.

My God! I'm thinking. There's steam going everywhere, steam all over this goddamn place—like nothing at all has happened, like it's just another one of those days, one day like all the rest.

Franny, he says, and stands straight up in his boxer shorts!

Rick, there's something I want to talk with you about, I start telling him again. There's something that's been on my mind—

He backs me straight into the counter and puts his hand around my waist. In no time, he grabs my ass and presses himself square into me.

Rick, I say. Did you hear me? Rick—

He slips his fingers beneath my underwear. He pulls my hair away from my neck, and kisses my neck. He starts pulling down my underwear.

I can feel myself going...

Lying in bed, I wake up to hear Rick talking on the phone in a low voice, and push myself up, *straining to listen.* Outside there's the sound of Mr. Carlson's back door swinging closed and a few minutes later the sound of the young girl's car pulling away.

When Rick walks back into the bedroom he's startled to see me sitting up in bed. He looks like he saw a ghost!

What's wrong? I say to him.

With what? he says and *squints* his eyes.

He crawls into bed, *hovers* over me and leans his body into mine.

He takes his hand along the side of my face but I shake him away.

He tries it again and I do the same thing. Eventually, he sidles himself off me.

10

All right, all right, he says. I guess I shouldn't push my luck. He laughs to himself and shakes his head. Then he grabs his boxer shorts from the floor. Then a pair of pants and a shirt from the closet. He slips his shoes on. First one, then the other.

I stay there watching him tie his laces. It's like I'm frozen! Part of me wants to make a run for it, part of me wants to just keep lying there. I don't know which part to believe!

So I close my eyes a moment. I put my hands over my chest and just lie there.

Well, he says, what are you waiting for? Are you ready or what? Are we going to do this?

He says, I told this lady we'd be there by noon. He tells me she's got another person interested in the car, and she doesn't care who she sells it to.

Typical woman, he says. There's no loyalty there. She's made no promises to nobody!

From where we live to get to where we're going, you take Churchill Road to Wolfpit, then a right onto Belden Hill for a while until you come to Al's Place, next to the old Shell Station which is a Texaco now. From there you take a left and head onto Route 7, where you keep going for several miles until you come to the stoplight at the four-way intersection at the end. If you go to the right a mile or so, you come to one town. Off to the left, the same thing happens. And straight ahead brings you to another highway, which leads to another set of connecting roads.

All my life Rick and I lived in the same town. We were high school sweethearts and when I got pregnant my senior year, we had certain notions. We were young and we were in love, we figured that was all you needed, and for a time maybe it was. We raised our family that way. We did the best we could. Sure, we made a lot of mistakes, but nobody died on our watch, as Rick's fond of saying.

He'd written down the directions. He said the old lady had given them to him over the phone, just before he'd come back to the bedroom, just before I'd started to question him.

But I don't know!

Which way now? he says to me.

We've driven on these roads a million times. The idea that we need directions is suddenly incredible to me. I can't even tell you how many times Rick's said he could damn near drive through every square inch of this town blindfolded and then come back twenty years later and do the same things in the dark.

I'm holding the directions, the directions that Rick wrote and came back to the bedroom with, shortly after I showered and cleaned myself and got dressed and he went back to the kitchen to make some more coffee.

I look down at my hand, and notice my fist is suddenly gripped tight around them, so tight that I can't even open it.

The light at the intersection turns green but I don't notice, not right away at least. I'm not paying attention. There are other things here!

You see, Rick was my one true love! For the longest time he was my everything!

Well? Rick says.

Well what? I say.

Which way, Franny? Which way are we going *now?*

He gives me this look but I don't know what to say to him.

Behind us, the cars start beeping, one after another, and I can feel my heart racing, I can feel my grip growing tighter.

Franny, Rick says.

He starts talking but it's like neither one of us is saying anything.

I look to my right, and then I look off to the left. I watch as the cars start toward me from the opposite direction. From the other set of connecting roads.

He puts the car in park, switches the hazards on, rolls down the window, sticks his arm out and waves the cars forward.

…Afterward, he starts up again! I try pulling away but he's forceful—

Look at me, Franny, he says. *Look at me!*

So I do.

I look at his eyes, his nose, I look at his chin. I start remembering what he looked like when we first started together all those years ago, when he was a senior and I was a freshman.

I have this picture!

I close my eyes, and all of a sudden it starts coming back to me.

It's all right, Franny, I hear him say. It's going to be all right. We've talked about this. You just have to trust me, you know?

Oh Franny, he says. I just wish I knew what you were thinking. He puts one hand on my leg, with the other he starts at my tears.

Rick—I get out. But that's all! Out of everything, it's all I can manage.

What Could We Have Possibly Known About Love Then?

He starts kissing my eyes, my cheeks, my lips. He starts pushing his tongue through and I open my mouth. I let him because I know. This isn't the first time. My mind's been made. Which as he does makes me cry all the more.

The Owl

I'd been in Chicago most of the spring. Two and a half months to be exact. Before that it was Boston, Philadelphia and Charlotte. There was Los Angeles and San Francisco, we did that run, Dallas too. We'd spent some time in Miami. About three weeks there. Miami, what a time we had. But who knows? Who or what's to say anymore?

After a while, all this time, all these stops and dinners, these late night meetings, all these things we do, well, they simply start to bleed into one.

To be honest, I was never particularly fond of traveling, flying out Monday morning, returning late Friday night. It wasn't anything I'd signed up for, at least. I'd known plenty of guys that couldn't get enough, especially the younger ones. But I'd never felt comfortable with it at any age. For one thing, there was that plane ride I took with my mother when I was sixteen and we went off to Florida during the eye of a storm to visit my Aunt Lauren, my mother's sister.

Why that plane ever took off in the first place is beyond me.

Besides, I was the creative type, that's what I'd been hired for anyway. Writing campaign pitches, stories and so on. Doing that made me feel as though my feet were solid to the ground. I was good at it after all.

But when Mr. Griffin called me into his office and told me about this team he'd put together—about a dozen of us from across the company *handpicked* for one reason or the other—what could I say, what choice did I have?

The Ryan Griffin Company, where I'd worked the last dozen years, was undergoing a period of significant change.

When our largest account decided to shake things up a bit and turn its business over to a direct competitor, things around here got interesting. There were grumblings at first, then talk of restructuring and consolidation, then the first wave of layoffs.

Maybe if it wasn't for the kids, I would have just up and quit. But who's to say that would have been right either? We'd known plenty of people that had been laid off or were concerned enough. And every time you turned on the news or listened to the radio someone was always telling you the economy was headed straight down the toilet.

There were tough roads ahead, tougher than this country had experienced in a long time. And there was no escaping it, no matter how hard you tried.

That night I answered the phone, I could tell right away that Alice was upset.

Alice, what's wrong? I said. Alice, honey. Dear, dear Alice.

We were both trying to keep our heads above water. This thing wasn't easy for either one of us. Chicago, all this traveling, it was like some great weight we carried.

Didn't I know it! Alice was the only woman I'd ever loved.

I know it's late, Alice said, I know you're probably exhausted, I know I shouldn't have called. But *God help me,*

16

The Owl

Marty, I was in a dead sleep, I was *nearly* knocked out cold myself, when all of a sudden here comes that noise again, that insistent knocking—*Hello, is anybody there?*—and it keeps on growing louder and louder...

I was half-scared out of my mind, Alice said. Marty, she said, when I woke up my heart was pounding, I could barely breathe. It's like they're on a mission, she said, every time I close my eyes, it's like they know—

What are you talking about? I asked her.

Who is it?

I didn't tell you? Alice said. I can't believe I didn't tell you. Marty, between the girls and *everything else* I've practically been up all night.

Alice said she'd run into Mike and the kids at the grocery store earlier that day, in the frozen food section of all places—

You should have seen him, Alice said. The way he looked, the way he was shuffling his feet like he didn't know one way from the other—

It just about broke your heart, she said. She said, It just about tore your heart in two.

We'd known Mike and Emily a long time, since the girls were little and Alice and Emily were volunteering at the grammar school together. In many ways they'd been our best friends in town here, and to see them going through things...

The light in the bathroom came on and there was the sound of running water and people singing loudly up and down the hallway, and I turned out of bed, put some clothes on and pushed open the door leading out onto the balcony.

Overhead a plane was going off in the distance. Traffic rushed up and down the street. A cab pulled in front of the hotel and a young couple stepped out.

Alice said she told Mike if he needed anything, *anything at all*—like someone to watch the kids or pick the kids up from school or even to just come over and watch the television and talk—we'd be there for him.

Anytime, anywhere, she said, our door was always open and not to think twice about it. Of course, I was in Chicago still—

So what did he say? I said.

The bathroom light clicked off and I turned back around and leaned over the rail.

…It was just *so* awful—Alice insisted.

Marty, are you still here?

I closed my eyes and opened them and watched the couple at the street below, the red taillights from the traffic getting closer and closer and then further and further out.

I started thinking about what my father said about the city life, the hustle and bustle, the chaos of it all, and felt everything go weightless at once.

Alice, it's going to be all right, I said. Try not to let it bother you. He's just going through a difficult time. Everything is going to work itself out, you'll see.

When are you going to be home? Alice said.

Honey, why don't you come back to bed?

I haven't been able to sleep all night.

At the street below the woman began to laugh and the man walked over to her and the two of them started dancing, and I could hear Alice's voice shaking on the other end, I could feel myself shaking.

The Owl

The city lights continued on and off and I could hear the sounds of heavy footsteps coming toward me and then a long slender arm starting around my waist.

Alice...I said.

Oh, here you are! she said.

And I just wanted to scream. I just wanted to scream into the telephone at the two of them as loud as I could.

Marty! Alice screamed. Marty! *My God, Marty,* you should have seen the way he looked at me!

I took a red eye from Chicago to LaGuardia that Friday night. As usual, there was the driver to take us from the airport. Most Fridays, Teddy Johnson from the New York office flew in with me. But he was staying through the weekend. He *said* he'd fallen behind on his end and needed to catch up. So Denise and I spent some time after the flight. We were both hungry. So we made a deal with the driver before Connecticut.

Denise said, If you don't mind? We hope we're not imposing.

I saw the driver flash his eyes in the rearview mirror and look between the two of us. First at Denise, and then at me.

But what did he care? I thought. *What else did he have to do?*

There was a twenty-four hour diner off the main highway with a gas station and motel and a small convenience market attached.

For one reason or another when we went inside I had the feeling I'd been there before and tried to explain it to the waitress to see if she knew anything.

What Could We Have Possibly Known About Love Then?

It was an old Western-style restaurant, I told her. Once, I think, when I was a little kid, we stopped here on our way back from Wappingers Falls.

I told her how the booths were set up then. How they had one of those old-fashioned cash registers in the front and a bunch of wagon wheels on the wall. I told her about that old shepherd that was just lying around in the middle of everything like a piece of old furniture.

I said how I thought the name of the place was Lee Simmons, probably after that old cowboy from the thirties and forties.

But our waitress didn't know anything about that. She said she didn't know anything about a dog or an old cash register and so on. Couldn't afford it, frankly. All she knew were the six months she'd been working this job, if that. To tell the truth, she said, that was all the time a person had for these days.

Then she said, Do you know what you want or what?

Denise started to explain how we'd just come back from Chicago and how before that it had been another place and how in a few weeks probably it would be somewhere else. But you could tell the waitress wasn't looking for that.

So I gathered the menus and ordered a hamburger and Denise ordered the turkey club. We both had drinks. Halfway through the meal, Denise went over to the jukebox and put in a few quarters.

When I got home that morning, Alice and the girls were sleeping and I went into the hall bathroom and cleaned up. I took a shower and changed my clothes. I started a load of laundry.

The Owl

I went into the kitchen and made some coffee and looked around. I looked in the family room, the dining room. I came back and read through the *To Do* list stuck to the refrigerator, the bills that had been piling up on the kitchen table.

It looked like nothing had changed from the week before. Everything was just as it had been, just as it would be, I figured, weeks from now.

After some time I went out to the porch and sat awhile.

I'd been carrying a photograph of my father in my wallet ever since my mother died this past November and we'd cleaned out the house getting it ready for sale. We were all there, me and my sisters, my sisters' husbands, Alice was there too.

It was Alice who'd found the photograph when we were going through things.

I was standing in my childhood bedroom looking at the old wallpaper, an old desk lamp, trying to decide what to do with everything, when Alice raced in and held this photograph to the side of my face and said something my mother used to say when everyone was still alive.

She said, There's no denying where you came from, that's for sure.

Martin, she'd say, nobody's ever going to mistake you for the milkman's son.

I looked at the photograph and studied my father's face. I thought about the things I knew, the things I didn't know. *He was just around my age now.*

In the photograph he was sitting in his old terrycloth chair, he had his feet kicked up. He wore an old plaid shirt, blue jeans and white socks. He had a beard started. He was carrying a drink in his right hand, the television clicker in the other. He looked like he'd just come home having worked an entire month straight. It wasn't like anything I knew. He didn't even look to put up a fight. He just stared straight ahead. It was like by that time he was already gone.

Mostly, I remember, when my mother started with her new camera, he'd put his hands up to his face and start complaining like hell about it. He'd make such a fuss.

God damn it, Rose! We're just trying to relax here—

And my mother would just look around and smile, pretending she didn't hear anybody or anything anyone was saying. Like maybe she didn't care, or maybe she didn't want to know.

She'd just look through her viewfinder and tell us all to pipe down. She'd say, *You two* just keep quiet, *you two* stop squirrelling around. Hold still, *you two,* will you?

But it hardly mattered. It seemed as though something would always end up happening nevertheless. Like the light would suddenly shift, causing the picture to go all out of focus. Or someone would move like the wind rustling through the trees and end up missing a hand or a leg or the tops of their heads for it.

My father would have a field day but my mother was always so calm.

You complain now, she'd say. You complain and complain but one day you'll be happy for it, one day you'll thank me. One day when I'm long gone, when I'm dead and buried and you're all crying at my gravesite, missing the hell out of me, you'll be happy to have something to remember how things were, to remember how we were once too—

The Owl

The sun started to lift from just behind the trees and I sat there trying to locate that night my father and I stayed at the local Howard Johnson's when my sisters were having a large sleepover with the Girl Scouts, and no one thought it was fit to have either my father or me around interfering.

Not that either one of us cared a damn.

It was so goddamn loud in there listening to all that nonsense about nothing in particular that a man could just about lose his wits.

That night at the Howard Johnson's we'd ordered two large pizzas with pepperoni and anchovies and watched an old movie with Steve McQueen on the television. My father'd brought a cooler of Pabst Blue Ribbon and we'd had a few beers each. I'd just turned fifteen years old.

That was the night we talked about Montana, a trip my father was thinking about taking the end of *that* summer to visit an old friend, an old army buddy named Bill Henson, who lived in a small house on good fishing grounds.

Just Bill and his son, living the good life.

The fishing around here isn't bad, my father would say, especially when one of us would pull in a nice striper. But wait until you see the fishing in Montana. It's a whole different world out there. Montana, he'd say, that's the real deal.

I took a deep breath and finished my coffee. Returned my father's photograph to my wallet, got up and stretched and started for the garage.

That night she called Alice said she'd hardly be surprised to come home the next day and find a thousand woodpeckers going at our furniture. It's like they're trying to bore a hole straight in, she said. Like they know there's something here all right, something to get their claws on.

Alice said she couldn't remember the last time she'd had such a terrible dream, a dream she hoped she would never have again. A house full of woodpeckers, she said, everywhere you turned, attacking the dining room table and chairs, the kitchen countertops and cabinets. Coming through the hardwood floors and raising hell in the girls' rooms, our study, even our bedroom.

And there was nothing she could do to stop them.

In the dream, she said, she tried to take a broom. She tried a fire extinguisher, loud music even. But nothing worked.

It was like the more she tried, the worse it got. Like there was no way of turning back what had already been done.

I opened the garage door and started moving things around.

I could see the ladder behind a bunch of boxes from my mother's house in the corner, and I took a few steps forward and began pulling them out one at a time gently so as not to break anything.

I read over Alice's handwriting, which was all over, and stood there looking at the boxes and the cars, the kids' bicycles, the things we'd accumulated over the years.

Eventually I rustled the ladder out. *I nearly pulled my back doing it!*

It had been quite some time since I'd found myself in the camping section of Herman's Sporting Goods Store. A few years ago, after things had come out, Alice thought it'd be a good idea if we took off and spent the week at the local campgrounds. At first, Alice'd suggested leaving the kids behind. Her sister had offered to watch the kids, her mother even.

Maybe it'd be best for just the two of us to get away. Maybe that would be better, Alice said.

Maybe it would be, I thought then. But maybe it wouldn't too. Maybe we should take them. Maybe *that* would be better, I thought. Maybe it'd be better if they'd come along.

What did I know from these things?

When we decided to go for sure, that we were going to do this, I called the local rental and got us an RV and a canoe for the week. Then I went down to Herman's and purchased some poles, fishing nets and tackle boxes for the kids. I purchased some sleeping bags too, a small propane grill even.

Alice said those days I was like a kid in a candy store, buying one thing, then another. She said she hadn't seen that side of me in a very long time. I looked so happy, she said. She said it was so nice to see.

But I never knew what she meant by that. It was *puzzling* really. I'd always figured I was happy enough. After all, I wasn't the one who'd carried on like I was unhappy then.

We did some fishing that week. We took the canoe around the lake. We toasted marshmallows and made S'mores and Alice and I traded off stories for the kids' entertainment. At night we all slept in the RV. A few rainy afternoons we watched movies there too. It wasn't anything like I'd remembered camping to be, but the kids had a good time, and Alice and I got our chance.

The salesman returned from the stockroom with a box tucked under his arm. He came over to where I was standing and put the box on the counter.

This must be your lucky day, he said to me.

I looked up at him. He was a bright-eyed young man with long thick hair and a beard coming in. He had his whole life in front of him, I thought. The world was his oyster.

If you can believe it, he said, this was the last one we had in stock.

I pushed at my own thinning hair, and looked down at the box and picked it up. The Owl, it said.

I read over the label. The name of the manufacturing company. Where that Owl had come from before here.

We get these special from a company out in California, he said. A fella was here last fall.

My phone started vibrating, and the salesman put the box in a Herman's shopping bag with the receipt and handed it to me.

I thanked him and went a few aisles over and took out my phone and stood there a moment, pretending to be looking for something else.

At the end of the aisle a father was standing with his son, the two of them going through a bunch of rods. I brought the phone to my ear, bent my head and listened.

I can't wait, I heard the boy say.

Try this one on for size, the father said.

He handed the boy the rod. Then took it and handed him another.

In between, the boy flicked his wrist.

How does that feel? the father said.

It feels good, the boy said.

It's not too heavy, is it?

The Owl

By the time I found her, Alice was sitting on a bench at the other end of the store, not all that far from the entrance where there was a short waterfall spilling into a small pond with a short bridge over the center.

She'd seen me walking over and smiled and stood. I looked down at the bench covered with the girls' spring jackets and a few Herman's shopping bags.

How did you make out? I said to her.

Yesterday, on the car ride home from soccer practice, Lindsey had said that Coach Warner, *Coach Wormser* as she called him, had made a stink about her not having her shin guards. She hadn't had them all week apparently. She'd lost them. Where she'd lost them, she didn't know. Maybe she'd lost them at school, maybe they were at a friend's house, maybe she'd misplaced them at home. And what difference did it make anyway? All she knew was that *Wormser* told her if she was going to play during Sunday's game—which she said she could give a rat's ass about—then we needed to take her to get shin guards.

They'd gotten Lindsey shin guards, Alice said. Shin guards and sneakers, sneakers for both of the girls. First, it was Carol who needed sneakers, and because Carol needed sneakers, well, Lindsey had to have a new pair of sneakers.

What's fair is fair, right? Lindsey said.

I can't believe how exhausting it is trying to keep up with these girls, Alice said. She took a deep breath and leaned into me.

Where are they now? I said.

They ran into some friends. *Boys,* Alice said.

Boys? I said.

Alice nodded her heard. She pulled back and looked up at me.

What Could We Have Possibly Known About Love Then?

She said, You should have seen the look on your daughter Lindsey's face when I tried to introduce myself.

Alice tried to make that face. I'd seen that face all right.

Sometimes I feel like I'm constantly walking on eggshells around that girl, Alice said.

I don't know how you do it, Alice, I said.

It's not easy, she said. Try keeping her off the phone at night, or getting her to concentrate on her homework—

Maybe I could talk with her, I said. Maybe that would do something.

Alice shrugged her shoulders. She leaned her head from one side to the other.

Anyway, she said. How did *you* make out? Did you find what you were looking for? Did you explain *our* situation? Did you tell them about the pecking at the eaves, and how much they've been keeping us all up at night?

She put her hand on my arm and I spread the bag open and removed the box and handed it to her.

She looked at the box. The Owl? she said.

It should scare them off, I said. I said, It's something my father did once when we were younger.

She said, Do you *really* think this will work?

Alice began fooling with the box and I walked a few feet over in the direction of the pond and looked at the small lights reaching into the dark water, some of the plants at the edges, the bubbles that were making their way to the surface.

Alice said she saw me talking to Greg Collins earlier.

Greg Collins was one of the parents in town we knew through the girls. Greg and his wife Karen. They had a son and a daughter. Carol, our eldest, was friends with his daughter Erin.

What was he doing? Alice said.

Nothing much, I said. He was just getting things for the kids. He had his son with him.

Did he say anything about Mike? Alice said. I mean has he run into him? Did you tell him I saw Mike at the grocery store? Has Karen said anything about Emily?

I looked around the pond. I was happy we were the only ones there.

What's there to say? I said.

I turned around and looked at Alice, and she shrugged her shoulders and shook her head in agreement. She took a deep breath. It's just so horrible, you know?

I nodded my head and reached for the box. I removed The Owl from the box and held it outstretched, in front of the two of us.

So what do you think? Alice said. It's pretty scary-looking, isn't it?

She looked at The Owl. She tried to make her eyes go just as wide. Then she took The Owl's head and spun it all the way against its swivel neck, and then let it go, so that its head went back and forth, its yellow eyes bobbed up and down.

So this should work then? she said. *This* will drive them away?

It should, I said.

Thank God, she said. Marty, she said, I can barely sleep at night.

She took The Owl and then she gave it back to me, and I returned it to its box, then the box to the bag, just as it had been given me before.

What Could We Have Possibly Known About Love Then?

I tied the handles of the bag together. Then untied them. Then I tied them again.

I looked back at the pond, then at Alice and tried to remember things.

For some reason it was important for me to get this right.

Alice said, Sometimes when I think of what happened, the decisions I made, and I think of everything I must have put you through—

I put the box on the bench and looked at her, and Alice looked down at her shoes. Then she looked away and hesitated a moment.

Alice, I said, we've talked about this. We've been through this already. What's the point of going through this again?

I just don't know how you ever forgave me. I just don't know what gave you the strength.

You didn't do anything to deserve how I treated you then, Alice said. Marty, she said, I don't know what the hell I was thinking. He didn't mean anything to me. None of that meant anything…

I said, Alice, please—

But she started to say things, even more things.

These were things I didn't need to hear again.

So I walked over to her. I put my hands on her head and smoothed her hair. I said, You can't do anything about the past, didn't we say that? The past is the past, isn't it? Alice, we agreed, didn't we?

I said, Alice, listen to me…

Alice lowered her head. Her eyes had started to well.

Marty…she said.

The Owl

Then I said: Are you going to help me or what? Isn't that what you said? You said you'd help me, didn't you?

Alice, I said, c'mon.

I grabbed her hand and walked over to the line of red machines filled with fish food. For all I knew they were the same red machines that had been there when I was a little kid. At least they looked old enough.

I put my hand in my pocket and dug through the change I had leftover, and put two quarters in each of two machines, a plastic cup from the dispenser beneath each chute, and turned the cranks, one at a time.

Here, I said, and handed Alice the two plastic cups.

What about the girls? Alice said in between tears. Should we wait for the girls?

I looked around. We both did. We looked from here to there. We didn't look all that much.

Forget about them, I said.

Alice nodded her head and wiped just beneath her eyes. She reached into her purse for a Kleenex and blew her nose.

Then she said, Marty, where do you want me to start pouring?

It doesn't matter, I said. Just make it around. I showed her what I meant with my hands. It was the same thing we'd talked about on the car ride over—

I walked to the edge of the pond where the bridge started and read a sign about young children being accompanied by a parent to ensure their safety.

I didn't remember ever seeing a sign like that before. But things were different then, I thought.

My phone started vibrating again and I reached into my pocket and turned it off. Then I grabbed the rails and walked toward the center.

This whole thing, it was Alice's idea, I told myself.

I looked around the store. I looked over to where the athletic equipment was, where I'd seen Greg and his son earlier, then off to the camping section again.

From where I was standing it was like I could see everything.

I thought about the dreams I'd had when Alice and I first met, and the dreams I'd had before that, when I was younger.

I thought about that time I heard my father telling my Uncle Bill: *You take a man who's lost sight of himself and turn him inside out, and you'll see how there's nothing left to him that resembles any part worth living.*

Marty, do you want me to start now? Alice said.

I tightened my grip on the rail, leaned over some and looked straight down into the water. I thought about Mike and Emily, and how during the dark days Alice had called them the great beacon of hope, the people other people could lean on when they were trying to find their long way back home.

I took a deep breath and watched a few fish go by, then the water go back and forth, then no fish at all. I could see my reflection waving.

All right, I said. Go ahead.

I never did make it out to Montana with my father. A few months after we'd started to make plans, there was an accident at work. Something to do with the machinery my father had been operating nearly the entire time I was alive. The machinery, he was proud of saying, he could operate in his sleep.

After the accident an investigation determined my father had been standing too close to the edge, that he'd disregarded the manufacturer's instructions on the label stuck to the machine.

The manufacturer claimed my father's negligence was the reason he got caught up in the jaws. My mother said, They had their reasons—

There were other claims too.

Within a few weeks of burying my father, rumors started around town that my father and Donna Jackson, Peter Jackson's wife, had been having an affair, and that maybe *that* was the cause of it. Some people said Peter Jackson, who'd worked the machine next to my father's, had pushed him into it. Peter had found letters, people were saying, letters where my father proposed that he and Donna make a run for it, move out someplace where the air is clean and leave everything else behind.

But if that was true, neither Peter nor Mrs. Jackson ever came forward, and no letters were ever produced.

And when I'd say something to my mother about it, she'd merely laugh it off. Your father a writer? she'd say.

Well, certainly there was some truth to that.

As you can imagine, after my father passed things seemed to get a whole lot worse before they got any better. Harold was one of those things. I knew he made my mother happy, and he tried. But that hardly meant anything to me.

Sometimes, when I was *really* getting uncontrollable, I suppose, Harold would stop coming by for a while, and my mother and I would start spending more time together.

What Could We Have Possibly Known About Love Then?

On some of those days we'd come down to Herman's, *just* my mother and me. We'd go shopping and talk through things. We'd talk about my classes, the books I was reading. We'd talk about the baseball season and what I planned to major in in college.

Sometimes we'd sit by the pond and just talk about my father. It was important, my mother would say. It was important for me, yes, but it was important for her too. There were certain things she needed me to know.

For one thing, she'd tell me she cared for Harold, Harold was a wonderful man, she'd say. But he'd never be your father. Nobody will ever be your father, she'd say. Not that big old bullfish, always bulling his way over just about anything.

Alice had gone around the pond, sprinkling the fish food just like I'd shown her. Then she walked up the short bridge and came alongside me. I was leaning over the rail still, looking into the water.

What are you thinking about? she said.

Nothing, I said. But it wasn't true.

For a moment I thought about my mother and how I'd never see her again and how much I loved her. For months now, ever since she died, I'd been trying to remember her as she was, before the last few years, before the Alzheimer's had set in.

Standing there, I remembered this one time she poked her head out the kitchen window when I was just a little kid, and called to me.

I'd just come back from fishing with one of the neighbors down the street.

34

I thought about things like that.

Alice put her arm around my back and leaned her chin into my shoulder. A few more fish swam by and there was the outline of the two of us in the water waving.

You know what we should do? Alice said.

I looked at her. I didn't say anything. I let her go on. I didn't interrupt her at all.

The way I figured it, I'd go back to Chicago just like I'd planned. Maybe that girl and I would have one last go around, maybe we wouldn't. In either case, I'd iron things out there, and then I'd call Mr. Griffin to set up a meeting.

Even with the economy the way it was, I'd tell him what a toll all this traveling was starting to take on my family. I figured he'd understand.

Love Stories

They were having dinner at Dominick's restaurant downtown—this boy and this girl, this boy's parents and this girl's parents—celebrating the boy and girl's recent engagement, trading stories and laughing.

Love stories, the girl's mother had called them at one point, though the girl was not entirely sure.

First, it was the girl's mother who went; then the girl's father and then the boy's father.

When the girl's father raised his hand to signal the waitress for another round of drinks, the boy put his arm around the girl's shoulder and smiled and the girl looked up at him and blushed.

Isn't that adorable? the girl's mother said.

Look at them, the boy's mother said. Look at the two of them. Look at how young and happy and beautiful they are.

They had spent all morning until late that afternoon driving practically from one end of the state to the other—between reception halls and churches, past a handful of places where the girl's mother had thought maybe they could take pictures after the ceremony.

It had seemed like a lot to think about all of a sudden (especially since they'd been engaged less than a month), the boy and girl laughed as they walked through the big, empty spaces of the *Patterson Hotel* and the *Riverview,* the *Water's Edge* and the *Inn at the Villa Bianca* and tried to imagine a room full of two hundred and fifty of their closest family and friends.

But both the girl's mother and the boy's father agreed that if they were going to marry next summer like the boy and girl had wanted, then there were certain decisions they needed to make right away. (Like where to hold the wedding reception, for instance, and the ceremony; and what they'd planned on doing with out-of-town guests, etc.)

And other decisions they could make more leisurely in the months to come.

You could always elope, the girl's father joked once when the girl's mother was out of earshot. Save us all a hell of a lot of time, *and money!*

What was most important, the boy's mother said, just as her mother had reminded her, was that they'd always remember why they've decided to marry in the first place; that in spite of everything that may come to pass, they'd fight to the very end to hold onto what was so special between them.

...And so, I handed each of them a knife, the girl's mother said, *the two kids and Frank, and threw myself on the floor all stretched out for everyone to see, and said, 'Now here's your chance, here's the main event, here's what everybody's been waiting for—'*

What Could We Have Possibly Known About Love Then?

It was a beautiful night. Clear, with a big yellow moon out and a myriad of bright stars.

After dinner the boy's father suggested that maybe the two fathers and the boy spend the next Saturday golfing the *Racebrooke Country Club,* where the boy's parents were members, while the women spent the day in the city, looking at wedding dresses and getting ideas for the floral arrangements—just like the mothers had talked about. And then afterward they could meet again for dinner at Dominick's or maybe that new French bistro on the corner of Sanford Street that the girl's mother had been dying to try.

How does that sound to *you,* honey? the girl's mother said to the girl.

What do you say, *Champ?* the boy's father said to the boy.

On the way home the boy reached for his cigarettes and lit one. He searched the radio and rolled down the window, feeling the wind rush through his hair, while the girl kicked off her sandals and yawned.

I think that went *really* well, the boy said. I think everyone had a good time, don't you?

You sure you're all right to drive? the girl said.

I'm all right.

Because I can drive, the girl yawned.

I hardly had anything to drink.

Because the last thing I want to do is to get into an accident.

The boy tightened his grip on the steering wheel and the girl closed her eyes and opened them and turned her head and yawned and looked up at the boy.

Are you tired? the boy said.

I'm *so* tired, the girl said. I can't believe how tired I am. I don't know what it is, the girl said and reached her hand up to her mouth.

Long day, the boy said.

What? the girl said.

The boy lowered the radio. A lot to think about, you know?

He looked at the girl, and then up ahead at the big yellow moon.

But it seemed like everyone had a good time, he said. It seemed like our parents got along really well.

You see, the boy said, I told you there was nothing to worry about. Didn't I?

The boy drew on his cigarette and the girl nodded her head.

I hope so, the girl said.

You don't think? the boy said.

Hey, the boy said, did you hear the people behind us laughing?

When they got to the apartment, the girl went to the bathroom to brush her teeth and get ready for bed and the boy walked into the kitchen to grab himself a beer.

At the street below there was the sound of a young woman's voice and the boy moved toward the window wondering if maybe it was the girl in apartment 4A named Claire or the woman he'd just met from San Francisco who'd moved into 1C about three weeks earlier (where the old woman with the cats used to live, right next door to Tom and Nancy Newman).

She was quite good-looking, the boy thought, the girl from 1C—*and the girl from 4A for that matter!* Though they were very different looking girls.

Not that that meant anything. Not that any two girls are exactly the same. Or all that different too.

What Could We Have Possibly Known About Love Then?

The girl in 1C was tall and skinny, the boy recalled, with small breasts and dark hair, while the other girl was blonde-haired and blue-eyed with much larger breasts.

A nice full B-cup or even a good C, the boy thought. One or the other.

Probably, he'd thought, if he had to choose—from among the two of them, that is—he figured he'd take the girl in 1C because she had a nicer nose; and, *although he wasn't entirely sure,* he had the idea that maybe she was an artist, like a painter or a sculptor, and he'd always wanted to date an artist though he wasn't an artist himself.

It was strange, the boy knew, but he had always thought he could learn something from a girl like that. Though he didn't know what it would be exactly.

In either case, both girls were pretty good-looking, the boy believed. *One or the other,* the boy thought. Either way a guy could hardly go wrong.

The boy opened the refrigerator door and started shifting things around.

When the girl came out of the bathroom, the boy was sitting on the couch with a can of beer and the remote control.

What are you doing? the girl said as she walked into the television room.

Trying to find a movie. Do you want to watch a movie?

You don't want to go to bed?

I'm not tired, the boy said. I don't know what it is but I'm wide awake all of a sudden.

I can't believe how tired *I* am, the girl said.

Are you going to bed?

Not if you're not going. I don't want to go if you're not going. You know what I mean?

The girl dipped her head. Then she arched her back and reached her hands out high. When the boy looked up at her, the girl took a few steps forward and posed.

Do you see what I'm wearing? the girl said.

The boy smiled.

Well, what do you think? the girl said. She shifted the weight of her small hips from the right to the left.

It looks good, the boy said.

Good? the girl frowned.

It looks great, the boy assured her. You look beautiful.

It's the white nightgown I bought for our first anniversary, you know.

I know, the boy nodded. I remember.

Do you like it still? the girl said.

I do, the boy said. He moved one of the pillows. Here—he said and scooted over.

And you *don't* want to go to bed?

In a little bit, maybe. Let me just finish this beer. Okay?

Okay, the girl said. But not too far. Come closer, she said.

How's this? the boy said.

The girl nodded her head and crawled onto the couch and lay down next to the boy.

So you're going to watch a movie? the girl said.

I'd like to, the boy said, if I could find one. Is that what you want?

I don't care, the girl said. Are you comfortable?

I'm all right.

The boy looked at the girl and smiled and then turned back to the television and drank his beer, and the girl put her feet into the boy's lap and rubbed them slowly back and forth against the boy's penis.

What Could We Have Possibly Known About Love Then?

That was some night, the boy said. *Day and night,* he said. Don't you think?

You don't mind? the girl said. You'll tell me if it bothers you, she said, and rolled onto her side, adjusting her feet still in the boy's lap.

It doesn't bother me, the boy said. I don't mind.

Are you sure? the girl said.

It's fine with me, the boy said and put his free hand on the girl's left foot and pressed down.

The boy sat there flipping through the television channels, drinking his beer, watching sports for a time and then the news. He put on a music video and then the *History Channel* and then a show about redecorating a home.

The girl had fallen asleep beside him and when she woke up the boy was sitting there staring at a picture of the seven-day weather forecast.

I thought you were watching a movie, the girl said softly, slowly opening her eyes.

I couldn't find one, the boy said. There's nothing on. Nothing worth watching anyways.

Should we go to bed *then?* the girl said. How long have I been asleep? What time is it?

The girl looked at the boy and yawned and started to push herself up. She ran the back of her hand along her eyes and yawned again.

Did I snore? she said. God, I hope I didn't snore. I know that sometimes you say I snore when I have too much wine.

I don't think you snored, the boy said.

He looked at the girl and sipped his can of beer and then turned back to the television.

Hey, he said, it looks like we're going to have good weather next weekend.

When did you start caring about the weather?

If we go golfing, the boy explained, and you go to the city—

Is that what we're doing?

Isn't that what everyone said?

I don't know, the girl said. Is it?

The girl rolled onto her back and spread her legs open a bit and the boy put his hand on the girl's knee and looked at her legs and began to make tiny circles around the tiny scar from when she was just a little kid.

What are you thinking about? the girl said.

The boy shrugged his shoulders. I don't know, he said. Nothing really, and sipped his beer.

So you think the night went well then? the girl said.

I think so, the boy said. I think everyone had a good time, don't you?

I was hoping they would. I was thinking they did, but then I had my doubts.

The girl started fussing with the bottom of her nightgown and the boy drained the rest of his beer and moved his hand up along the girl's thigh.

The girl said, You don't think my mother had too much to drink *then*—and my father? She said, I thought they were drinking way too much. You know how loud my mother can get when she drinks and how my father starts repeating himself.

And what about those stories? the girl said. What about that awful story about the time my father was painting the house and my mother came out yelling that supper was getting cold and if he didn't get off the ladder immediately how she was going to drop to her knees and pray to God almighty that the ladder would pull away from the house and my father would shatter his leg in about a million pieces.

I mean have you ever heard of such an awful story?

I thought it was funny, the boy chuckled.

You did? the girl said.

Didn't you?

The boy put the empty beer can on the table and wiped along his lips. Thank God for those bushes, he laughed, and turned toward the girl and took his fingers along the small razor bumps on either side of her light blue panties.

He said, *Jesus,* did you see how much my parents were laughing? And the couple behind us? I thought that guy behind us was going to bust a gut he was laughing so hard.

The boy moved his fingers carefully beneath the girl's blue panties and started along the short hairs toward the middle.

I don't know, the girl said after a while. I just don't know.

The boy looked up at her. What don't you know?

The girl arched her back a little and the boy put his free hand on the girl's right knee and then along her thigh.

I mean the whole night I kept thinking about something my aunt had told me a long time ago, the girl said, about being able to tell a lot about someone from the way his parents treat each other. And there your parents are always holding hands in public or cooking together or dancing in the living room, and here are my parents talking all night about how they've wanted to kill each other in nearly every way imaginable.

I mean God only knows what your parents must think of me, the girl said. *You know?*

When the boy did not answer, the girl sat up slightly and kicked with her feet until the boy looked up at her.

What is it? the boy said. What's wrong?

The girl tried to look deeply into the boy's eyes.

She knew she loved the boy. She knew she had loved him more than anyone she had ever loved before. But what did that mean? she thought. Would that ever be enough?

I wouldn't worry about it, the boy said at last. They love you, he said. You know that. They *adore* you. What do they say all the time? 'They don't know what they would have done if you hadn't come into *my* life.'

I know that, the girl said.

So what are you *so* worried about? the boy said.

I guess I'm not, the girl said. *No!*

The girl looked up at the ceiling and smiled. She dropped her head back into the pillow and closed her eyes and moved her legs closer to the boy.

She said, Do you remember that time we happened to be in your parents' neighborhood and it was late but we decided to stop by anyways, and when we did, we walked in on your parents kissing on the couch, and how embarrassed you were, and how you said they were always doing things like that...

But by that point the boy did not seem to be paying much attention—

Afterward, the boy lay in bed listening to the girl snore. For more than an hour he had tried to fall asleep himself but had too much running through his mind.

He had thought about the girl's mother, for one, and how good-looking she was, and how one time when they were alone together in the hot tub their feet had touched and when she looked over at him slightly embarrassed he got the firm impression that if he had wanted to, well, she was game. Though for all practical purposes, he understood, if not then…they would have to wait until the next time the girl and her father went to the grocery store, or down the street for ice cream—

Outside there was a noise and the boy reached down to the floor for his boxer shorts and t-shirt and went over to the window and looked past the large oak tree out front from where he could hear the sound of voices trailing and a swinging gate and a car motor starting in the distance just beyond.

Suddenly, he recalled that early spring afternoon he and the girl had met more than two years ago *now* when he was waiting for Janet Unger, his girlfriend-at-the-time. But he never told the girl that either.

He reached into his boxer shorts and squeezed his slightly-erect penis and walked down the hall to the kitchen and began shifting things around in the refrigerator again.

He grabbed another can of beer, along with a stick of white cheese, and moved into the television room and sat down and started flipping through the channels.

…All night long he had tried to forget. But more and more there was that look of horror on the younger man's face as the oldest child grabbed his father by the throat and the faithful mother had to come between them both.

(But, of course, he was only trying to protect her!)

The boy loved his father. *All men make mistakes,* the mother tried to assure him. But the boy wondered when the wounds would finally heal—

Love Stories

How dare you judge me! he could hear his father scream. *What could you possibly know about love? You are just a little boy! And she is your mother, yes! But she is also 'my' wife!*

When the girl found the boy more than an hour later, alone and staring into the dark, she crept up alongside him quietly and put her long, thin arms around the boy's heavy shoulders and said: What's wrong, sweetie? What is it? It's all right. You can tell me. I had a feeling you were upset. You were so quiet all evening. I know we're both scared, but whatever it is, I'm sure we can work it out.

What We Keep When They Go

When the mind fails the heart lifts
so that the music of our lives
radiates a perfection amid none of the false notes.
A means of nature compensating for nature.
Feeling as provender for that other feeling
so that faith and beauty may persist while
there is still time. What happens to all of us at some point,
Maryann believed, was simply the Lord's way
of casting mirrors for the light.
When I found her alone in the garden crying
a few days after her father died,
what made her so emotional, she said,
were the loud sounds the old chimes kept making
as they sang continuously with the birds
through the passing wind.

Ed's Diner

To Whomever Is Listening,
Will you please listen to me?
We've been over this a million times. More than I care to remember, you must understand. But every time I try to speak it's as though I haven't said a word.
Can you hear me? Am I speaking loud enough this time?
For a while I didn't hear anything from them. There was no interference on their part and I was allowed to keep my life.
But then something happened, something I do not know. And ever since that time, they will not stop coming around.
They come around in the morning, for instance, while I'm drinking my coffee and reading the paper. Or at night when I've taken with the news and a TV dinner.
I try to gauge them in order to anticipate, but most of the time, as I see it, there's no way of telling.
For all I know it'll be the middle of a warm Saturday and I'll be out in the yard mowing the lawn or planting May flowers when they start up the drive in their cruisers with the sirens going.
Or, as though they were trying to slip under the radar, in one of those unmarked cars even.
Either way I do not feel comfortable. This much is true.

What Could We Have Possibly Known About Love Then?

Before, if I had some warning, if I'd just come from the shower, let's say, I'd pull my bathrobe tight around me, wrap one end over the other like a cocoon and then loop the belt twice.

If I happened to be in bed and it was late enough, I'd pretend I was sleeping. I'd hold my breath and keep my eyes closed. Sometimes I'd yawn. Sometimes I'd even cry. I'd always go to this special place.

Gary said he'd spent plenty of time on neighborhood rooftops when he was a kid gazing out as far as the eye could see where nobody could ever find you.

My God, the pictures he could paint!

I just want to be left alone, I tell them. Please go away. I just want to sleep. Aren't you tired? It's late, isn't it? I just want to go to bed.

Please, I say, there's nothing here. I have nothing left to offer you. I've told you everything I need to know.

Do you hear me? I say, This is my only request.

But they keep knocking. Occasionally they ring the doorbell twice, I've noticed, just like the movies, but they're not fooling anyone.

They knock on my front door. Sometimes they sneak around back. I could be in the kitchen cleaning pots and pans, for that matter, when their dark shadows start toward me from just beyond the bushes.

Amy Richardson, they say, we'd like to have a word with you. Amy Richardson.

And when I don't answer, when I stand there frozen because I am reminded, they just keep it up. What do they care?

Amy Richardson?
I've determined there must be protocol to matters such as this one.

For one thing they're always sure to let me know I'm safe.
You're safe, they say. You have nothing to worry about. We're not going to let anything happen to you. We're one of the good guys. We're on your side. Ms. Richardson, they say, we understand.
But when I tell them I'm in the middle of something, that it's not a good time, that I've thought it over like they've asked and decided I cannot in good conscience be of any legitimate service to them any longer, that's when they come to the door and start in on the locks.
May *we* come in?
How many of them are you? I want to know.
And when I tell them I do not think it would be possible— *You need to leave me alone, I say*—they lower their voices and continue to go about their business.
We promise we won't be that long. Ms. Richardson, we just have a few questions for you. *Honey,* this is for your own good.

Lately, the officer with the mustache is the one who asks the questions, while the fair-skinned one, who does not have a mustache, takes out his little pad and pen.
He's the one who's been giving me these *dirty* looks that I've been talking about.
Before they did it just the opposite. That went on for months.

What Could We Have Possibly Known About Love Then?

I wonder what they want from me.

I tell them I don't have anything to add. When is this going to stop? My story hasn't changed. You're wasting your time. I've told you everything I know.

But they press, they keep pushing. They come right up to my face to where our lips are almost touching. Sometimes they're downright forceful.

They say they want to know about a girl. They show me pictures. They say there's an on-going investigation into *this* girl's disappearance.

When was the last time you've seen him? I want the truth. You need to tell me the truth.

But I've never seen this girl. What girl? I say. This girl doesn't look like anyone I'd know. Who is this girl? She is not familiar.

There is no other girl, is there?

Maybe you think I haven't talked loud enough. That I'm one of those people that whispers or writes letters and throws them away. But, I swear, none of what has been reported is truly as it seems, and if I've told them once, I've told them a thousand times…

And about this girl, what am I supposed to make of it? I have a feeling I could talk to everyone until I'm blue in the face.

These officers say they want to understand. It's not my fault. You do not need to worry. You're not in any danger. We're here to help.

Wouldn't you like your story to be told?

But to tell the truth, talking to them is just like talking to my mother.

Do you know my mother?
Maybe, they're incapable, I think. Or maybe they're just not all that interested. In either case, for once and for all, this has gone too far. I don't know how much more of this a person can *ultimately* take. I just want to be left alone. This has got to stop, do you hear me? I need for you to listen, can you do that? Because whether you'd like to hear about it or not this is all I know.

The last time I saw Gary we were sitting at Ed's Diner. It was late. We'd just finished with dinner when the waitress came over. Her name was Jodie Rae. I remember that now. She was a pretty girl, young. She was nineteen, maybe twenty years old. Skinny with high cheekbones, long brown hair and these bright green eyes.

At one point, maybe when he got enough courage, I wasn't sure, Gary told her he didn't think he'd ever seen anyone with bright green eyes like that before, and how he figured he wasn't the only one.

When I first walked into Ed's Diner, Gary was sitting at one end of the counter, facing the front door. He was wearing a baseball cap, a heavy jacket and jeans. He'd grown a beard and his hair long. When he came up alongside me we just stood there a moment looking at each other.

I looked at his face. I looked at his strong nose and thin lips. I felt my hands grow moist. I took a deep breath.

Gary said he was hardly surprised I didn't recognize him right away, that he was the one who'd noticed me first. He said it was like that night he walked up to me outside Captain's Cove where my cousin Stacey and I used to go line dancing.

Gary said, Do you remember how nervous I was?

What Could We Have Possibly Known About Love Then?

I said, Gary, where the hell have you been?

That night, Gary said, before I even knew he existed, he'd created our whole life story. We had the same story, he said. He said it was like me and him were cut from the same cloth, like we were two people made just for each other.

Then he pulled me close. There's something I want to tell you, he said.

What is it? I said.

…But it was dark and late and I was not expecting.

So how was everything? our waitress said. I see you've enjoyed the meatloaf, I see you've nearly licked your plate clean. Does *he* do that at home?

Our waitress smiled at Gary and then she looked at me.

Gary said he didn't think he'd ever had meatloaf like that in his entire life. Sure, he'd had some good meatloaf over the years. There was my meatloaf, for instance. Amy makes one hell of a meatloaf, Gary said. My mother gave Amy the recipe. But there was something about Ed's meatloaf he just couldn't stop eating.

It was like he hadn't eaten for days, Gary said and laughed.

I must sound crazy, and the waitress said, You don't sound crazy at all.

She said Ed had built a reputation around that meatloaf, he'd become a celebrity of sorts in this small town here.

In fact, just a few months ago, she said, one of the city food critics wrote an article all about it with a picture of Ed working at the grill and everything.

You should have seen how excited he was, our waitress said, lifting her shoulders and rolling her head along her neck where she had a tattoo of a butterfly which wrinkled some and looked as though it was flapping its wings.

She said ever since that article people have started to come to Ed's from all over, not that Ed's wasn't busy before. Just last week, she said, a couple had driven nearly two hours in the middle of the night because the wife was pregnant and she'd heard about Ed's fried chicken from a friend of hers.

You want to talk about crazy, our waitress said.

Well, good food brings good people. That's for sure, Gary said.

That's what Ed always says.

The waitress reached over the table for Gary's plate and utensils and Gary handed her the empty side dish of mashed potatoes and the empty basket of bread and butter, the small condiment bottles from the center of the table.

He thanked her and looked at me and kept his eyes steady when she leaned over the table to wipe it down and her blouse pulled away from her chest some which is one of the things about Gary I think you should know.

You see, out of everyone I've come across in this life, Gary was the one who had the most *terrific* manners.

He was always thanking people, for instance, and smiling, and holding the door open no matter how long people took.

I have to admit sometimes it would get awfully frustrating. Especially if we found ourselves in a hurry. *C'mon Gary, we need to go!*

But when it came to certain types of people like the elderly, like an old blue-hair with a cane and a severe limp, for instance, there was nothing that Gary wouldn't do. It was like he could spend all day.

What Could We Have Possibly Known About Love Then?

Just take your time, he'd insist. You don't have to rush on my account. I have all the time in the world. I'm not going anywhere. Where am I going?

…Which, as I write this letter you've been asking for, makes so much of what I've been needing to tell you so very difficult to say.

It's like I tell everybody at one point, Gary had built us a home in Galveston, a small house that we'd made into a home, a home filled with everything that a girl like me could ever want, and we'd talked about filling that home with kids. I said two would be fine, a boy and a girl, that would be good enough. But Gary said he wanted at least three or four, maybe an even half dozen.

An even half dozen, my God. But you should have seen that house with only one toilet and a half of a bedroom that was shared with the kitchen.

I'd tell him: Gary, how could we have six children in that house? Where would everyone fit? A family of four would be a tight enough squeeze, I'd say. But Gary'd say, We'd manage. He'd say, There'll always be enough room in our house. Our house was a home after all.

Of course, my mother says she always knew there was something wrong with Gary. From the first time she laid eyes on him, she says, it was like he was too good to be true. *But what does she know? What did she ever care to know?* And when somebody's like that, Amy, she says, it's so easy for a person to get all mixed up.

"Just take your time, Ms. Richardson. Let's go over this again."

Amy, I am your mother! I need to know what happened! Tell me what happened! Tell me what that horrible man did to you!

And so we finished dinner, as I've said. Gary had ordered pie and coffee for the two of us. Though to be fair I told him I was on a diet. People were moving in and out and there was *this* one couple in particular who kept falling all over the place just two booths down from where we were sitting. (I don't think I've told you about them before. I don't think it dawned on me until just now that this might be something of interest.)

The man was leaning over the table, you see, and I kept looking at the girl. But then somebody went over to the jukebox and the waitress told us not to pay them too much mind. It was an old song by Kitty Wells. *It Wasn't God Who Made Honky Tonk Angels.*

So we got ourselves out of the booth. We went over to the jukebox and wrapped our arms around each other so tightly that it just about broke your heart. There was Patsy Cline and Red Foley and Loretta Lynn and "all my life I've lived with strangers and now my true love leaves again."

It's like I told the police, you understand: When news came that Gary's partner Ron had fallen off the roof and was killed, you should have seen how distraught Gary was because Ron should have never been on that roof in the first place. Yes, Ron was a good finish carpenter, there was no one better, but when it came to the rest of what had to be done, it was Gary *alone* who could dance on those roofs.

Besides, Gary loved Ron and Ron loved Gary. Yes, they fought from time to time, but *mostly* you should have seen the way the two of them could carry on. Like brothers, I'd say.

Like real family. And you don't do something like that to your
brother, do you?

"Well, which one is it?"
"I don't understand."
"You said you were the only ones there…"
"Yes."
"But a minute ago you said people were moving in and
out."
"Yes."

…I remember the door opening slowly. I remember
hearing a loud noise and the light falling in, a strong wind
breaking and the sound the tall trees made outside.

If you can imagine I remember strangely thinking that
someone somewhere was making the sign of the cross while
everything went dark awhile and people stumbled in and out
from the rowdy bar across the street just the same.

Gary was watching the television above the counter. I
drank my coffee and finished my pie. This much is true. I
begged him. *No,* I said. *Please,* I said. I can't, I told him. It
wouldn't be right.

But he moved his chair in. He looked around the room
(he'd been doing that all night) and put his hand on my knee
and then up along my thigh.

He said tomorrow or the next day, or the day after that, soon
enough anyways, there'd be all this talk coming from Virginia.
People saying he did something he didn't do. He said, You're
going to hear things, all these horrible things, they're going to
try to paint this picture, he said. But you know me better than

that. You know things about me that no one else knows. Gary said, You know the truth, don't you?

He had a plan. I wanted to get up and leave.

Amy! he said in this low tone, and my legs started to go light, my heart started to flutter.

He said in his eyes it would be me and him forever. Forever, he said, this whole thing would be our own little secret.

It was then the waitress came over and started to clear the plates. With the coffee cups going first and then the saucers, she wiped down the table and asked if we'd enjoyed the pie.

People ask me questions like that all the time but I hardly ever know what to say—

"You see, the more we fight to live, the more we find out we weren't the only ones."

From what I remember, she laughed unexpectedly. She snorted a great big belly laugh. She said something about "What's a young woman to do?" and putting on ten pounds herself just by looking at it.

And when she did, I noticed her heavy shoulders, the way her stomach fell endlessly from her shirt. Her dull eyes and short stringy hair.

At once I could see this look coming over Gary's face, I could see that young butterfly trying to flap its wings.

The whole time that first night I was lying in bed when I was just a little girl and my mother was at one of the neighbors' houses playing bridge and drinking wine and my father came to the bedroom door—

What Could We Have Possibly Known About Love Then?

I tried to stop him. *Mother, why won't you believe me?* But for the longest time I didn't know what to say, and then I heard an older girl cry...

Don't! I wanted to scream. Don't! She was so young, I thought, so beautiful! My God! We all were!

And so I closed my eyes—yes, it's true. And I lay my head back and squeezed his hands and felt his warm breath until there was nothing left and all the blood had drained out of him.

Amy...he said.

I could feel him all cut up and rough from calluses.

Amy...he said again.

I knew what these hands were capable of.

Yours Truly,
Kathryn Tobias Aranjo

We were in search of Heaven that summer, and simply too young to know it. The pretty girls, we thought, would always be that way. Night after night up to our waists in the cold New England waters—how small the shore houses seemed from where we stood.

Lantern's Point
H.T. Woods
1949

The Party

There was shit pretty much everywhere. Regardless where he looked there was no escaping it. The entire place had been turned over. When Mark arrived home he'd seen it just that way.

Piles of clothes spilling from the bedrooms out into the halls, into the bathroom where the vinyl curtain had been torn down, the shampoo bottles uncapped and knocked over, the faucet left running. There was water everywhere. In the kitchen, all along the countertops, on the tiled floor, the painted walls, was what remained of last night's dinner (grilled chicken, a side of rice, beets, a salad), the dinner before that and the entire contents of the refrigerator or so it seemed, and the small pantry too, dispensed like the paint of a Jackson Pollock painting.

In the dining room (where just the night before Mark and Cheryl had planned a long weekend to visit old friends they hadn't seen since they'd moved three hours south to Connecticut ten months ago) the floor was littered with broken china, candles and candlestick holders, the ceramic vase and flowers Mark had brought home a few days earlier "Just because…" and the large wine decanter Cheryl had purchased for the party they were having.

What Could We Have Possibly Known About Love Then?

When they first started talking about the party several weeks before, Cheryl had mentioned half a dozen teachers she planned on inviting. There were Bill and Ed from Mark's office and three of the women with whom Cheryl played tennis every Tuesday night, and their husbands—along with their instructor Dave. There was Cheryl's sister, Stephanie, who Mark wasn't particularly fond of, and Ted, the man she was "dating" at the time, and some of their friends.

There were the Petersons, *naturally,* and the Beckers, the Newmans and the Guilfoyles; the McLaughlins, etc. And the women in the book club had been talking about getting together for margaritas *anyway, so* maybe this would be the perfect time.

There was Cheryl's hairdresser Rita too, and the woman Cheryl had befriended recently who was a buyer for one of the big department stores in the city.

And, Mark, what do you think about that adorable couple we met at Roosters over the summer?

Of course, they couldn't ignore the handful of couples from the neighborhood for whom they had certain obligations, Cheryl said, due to proximity and what she called random acts of kindness.

There were Steve and Mary Dodge across the street, for instance, and Ken and Judith, their next-door neighbors. Kevin and Amy Clancy (who were the first to welcome Mark and Cheryl to the neighborhood) and the Walshs and Al Baker and his wife. There were Jim and Patty Emory and Sam and Cathy Myers and Tony and Liz.

But I thought we'd talked about this, Mark said. *I thought we decided, 'What if it rains? Where are we going to fit everyone?'*

The Party

And, of course, Cheryl had intended on inviting Tom and Beth. Of all the people in the neighborhood, Mark and Cheryl had been most friendly with Tom and Beth.

In the living room the stereo was playing still and Mark stared at it a minute listening. He took a deep breath and ran his hands through his hair and walked over to the front door and turned the knob and opened the door and closed the door and opened it again. He put his hand up to his mouth and leaned his head back and stared up at the ceiling where he could see a tiny cobweb starting in one corner.

He thought about getting a chair but then dropped his head and began working his thumb and forefinger against the bridge of his nose and across his eyes until he made stars.

My God! he thought. *How the hell did this happen? What the hell happened here?*

He walked over to the sofa and stuffed the cushions back into place. First one, then the other. Then he picked up the pillows from *Winchell's Department Store* which, he remembered, Cheryl had purchased for nearly eighty-five dollars apiece, and fluffed them out with both hands and arranged them according to memory. He reached for the green *throw* blanket and folded it. But then shook it out remembering and took two steps backwards and crossed one ankle in front of the other.

He put a finger up to his lower lip and pushed at his lip and wondered if it really did look better that way—the *throw,* that is—if it really did make a difference after all.

He had never given it much thought before *now*, that was true.

What Could We Have Possibly Known About Love Then?

He dropped one hand to his hip and tilted his head. He stood there a moment looking at everything.

Maybe it did look better. Maybe she was right. Maybe it really *does* matter in the end.

Am I losing my mind? Am I going crazy? What the hell! What the hell is going on here?

Outside the neighbor's dog started barking again and Mark walked out to the front porch and put his right hand up against the heavy glare of the sun as an unmarked van turned in from *Lewis,* started all the way down *Jennings* past the old grain silo (where Miller's Farm had been) before making a *decided* U-turn and doubling back slowly.

From where he was standing it was like he could see everything.

He could see Beth's car parked at the end of the driveway where it normally was, and *their* kids' toys scattered all around. Her front door was opened, along with one of the garage doors, Mark noticed. *Of course,* Tom's car wasn't there yet.

He thought about *that* time Beth called this past December when Tom was away and a snake had wrapped itself around the radiator pipe in *their* bedroom and she was sorry she called so late but didn't know what else to do.

Across the street Tony went around his yard with a large rake and a garbage pail. When he saw Mark he stopped temporarily and waved. He removed his oversized wicker sunhat and leaned his rake against the ashen trunk of a large oak tree and wiped at his brow as a line of wild turkeys started from the Myers' woods and a hen and her two chicks spilled onto the road.

The Party

At once the white van came to a halt and the driver rolled down his window, stuck his head out and, for a moment, appeared to look over in Mark's direction.

Mark scanned the long side of the van but there was no writing so it was difficult to tell. It could have been any number of things, he thought. He sat down on one of the *Adirondack* chairs Cheryl had purchased at a *Closeout* a few weeks before and tried to make himself comfortable. But couldn't. He grabbed at his chest and breathed slowly in and out. He felt his jaw go tight, his heart flicker. He stood up and watched the man open the door and turn slightly back toward him, the man appearing to nod his head and laugh as though perhaps he knew.

Mark opened his jaw and closed it. He watched Steve's dog go wildly back and forth along his electric fence. He couldn't believe what was happening.

My God, no! Mark said to himself. *Jesus, God, no! I thought we talked about this! I thought we talked this through! I thought we were square on this topic! What the hell! What the hell is she trying to do to me?!*

Mark was mulling things over when the phone started ringing. At first he didn't know if it was the phone ringing, the doorbell ringing, the stereo or what it was. It was like he was in a trance, like he didn't know what to believe, what not to believe.

He rubbed his eyes and forehead again. He ran his hands through his hair and yawned as the man stepped out of his van and proceeded to walk up to the Clancy's front door.

Mark was so tired. He couldn't believe how tired he was. Between work and everything else—that *goddamn* dog, for instance—he hadn't had a decent night's sleep in nearly a month.

The dog barked and Tony worked his way around to the back of his house and Mark grabbed a rock from the flower bed and thought about heaving it as hard as he could.

Inside he leaned over the telephone and looked at the number on the display. It was Cheryl calling.

My God, what now?! What on earth is it now?!

He went over to the front door and looked outside again. He leaned his head back and started to rub his forehead around each of his temples. He closed his eyes and opened them and noticed the spider's web had grown nearly five times the size it was just fifteen minutes before.

Jesus, God, Heaven Almighty!

When the phone started ringing again a few minutes later, he tried to level his voice but he could feel his hands shaking.

Hello, he said, hello…Yes, Cheryl, it's me. What is it? What do you want?

Mark had never felt himself prone to a heart attack. In fact, ever since he had graduated from college and stopped drinking and taking drugs and smoking and behaving *otherwise* recklessly, he had prided himself on maintaining good shape and being particularly *health*-conscious.

He was an active runner, for example. And both he and Cheryl spent a good amount of energy carefully selecting their food and preparing healthy dinners.

But all of a sudden a flash of pain started across his chest and he grabbed at it. All of a sudden he felt as though he had the constitution of a three hundred and fifty pound man, who'd been laid out flat by a thousand-pound weight.

The Party

...Well, if you can imagine, I was through the roof *really,* Cheryl said. Through the roof, I have to admit it. But then I called Stephanie. I called *you* first, Mark, but as we've already established, you weren't there. *So* I called Stephanie. To get things ironed out. Like pokers in a fire. You know how Stephanie talks, Cheryl laughed. You know how Stephanie's got her hand on the button where certain things are concerned. I mean what do I know about throwing parties? *I* don't know the first thing about throwing parties. But thank God for Stephanie. Out of all the people we know I knew I could count on Stephanie to help out. *Stephanie* is the real party thrower out of the group, I'll have you know, Cheryl said. Mark, Cheryl said, *Stephanie* has these things down to a science!

She said, Do you remember that one party she threw when she and her friends were living in Rhode Island and we'd first started together? *Heaven and Hell,* I think she called it. *Or something like that—*

Mark was sitting at the kitchen table staring *hopelessly* at a pile of *ungraded* school essays—titled *What I Did on My Summer Vacation*—which were now splattered with beet juice and rice and bits and pieces of grilled chicken, when suddenly all this commotion started coming through the phone. What sounded like people talking, music. What sounded like things getting shifted around.

At one point Mark could have sworn he heard what sounded like a fast-talking salesman say: *Do you like it? Do you like what you see?* And Cheryl shriek with excitement, then say: *You have no idea. That's exactly what I've been looking for.*

All of a sudden Mark's ears pricked up. In one deft movement he scattered all of the school essays to the floor. He looked at his watch and thought about catching a train. He remembered *that* conversation he and Cheryl had had just a few nights before about that antique auction in Kent and how Cheryl had promised not to spend a lot of money—she'd even agreed to *limits*.

Lying in bed that night, he recalled, he had tried to explain to her about last month's quarterlies, about the rumors that had started around the office. But, Mark, she'd said, you *just* have to trust me on this one. They're auctioning off the *cutest* pair of table lamps that would go perfectly with the décor I have in mind for the study.

Cheryl, where are you? Mark said. *My God, where the hell are you?* When are you coming home? Why don't you just come home, honey? *Forget about all that crap for God's sake!*

It's so dark in here, Cheryl said. I can't believe how dark it is. Stephanie never said anything about it being so dark.

Dark? Mark said. What do you mean *dark?*

My God, Mark, Cheryl laughed, I can barely see any of the merchandise.

Mark walked over to the sink and turned on the faucet. He reached into the cupboard for one of the few unbroken glasses and thought about biting off the rim. He poured himself a glass of water and leaned his head back but took too much water too quickly and began choking. He looked at the glass and cocked his arm.   He   nearly   slipped   on   a   piece   of   chicken. *Motherfucker!* He placed the glass on the countertop and began pounding at his chest. He turned on the faucet again and stuck his head in the sink and swished some water in his mouth and spit it out and watched it dribble down his chin. He looked at his reflection in the window above the sink and wondered if he was becoming delirious.

What's going on over there anyways? Cheryl said. What's all that noise? Mark, what is that? It sounds like gun shots over there. It sounds like people dancing. Are you all right? What's happening? Is everything *okay?*

There was a rush of excitement coming through the phone and he sat back down and tried to explain it to her.

He said, The money. The money. We don't have the money.

What? Cheryl said. What? Mark, I can barely hear you. Are you still there, sweetie? Can you hear me? God, it's so noisy in here, she said, you wouldn't even believe it. What did you say? What was it you were trying to tell me?

He looked at the phone. He rolled his head along his shoulders. He thought about what his father called "the thin lines of distinction" and wondered what he'd do if there was actually a cord.

The money, he said again. The money. We don't have any goddamn money.

What, Mark? Cheryl said. What? Mark, *honey,* I can't hear you. You'll have to speak a little louder—

He threw over a chair. He kicked a broken bowl across the room.

The money! he screamed. The money! He grabbed the glass off the counter and heaved it. What don't you understand?! We don't have any *goddamn* money!

It was starting to get dark out. The lights at the street were sputtering on and off. Mark had cleaned up the house and was bringing the last of the trash down by the curb. It just so happened the next day was garbage pick-up.

He moved one of the trash cans a few inches closer and looked over in the direction of Tony's house where a large aggressive turkey was showing its feathers, and then off in the distance, behind the Myers', where the sun was going behind the trees, illuminating here and there the large, oval-shaped silhouettes.

Every night, just around this time, about an hour before dark, they'd come together, these packs of wild turkeys, from all over the neighborhood, about seventy-five of them in all, before roosting in the trees behind Sam and Cathy Myers' house.

Last spring, after they'd first moved in, Mark remembered, Cheryl had counted as many as forty-seven turkeys at once.

Across the street Mark's neighbor Steve was standing in his yard smoking a cigarette. He waved but Mark pretended as though he hadn't seen him.

All I want is some peace. Just a little bit of peace and quiet. Is that too much to ask?

Mark liked Steve. In every sense of the word, Steve was a good neighbor. But for one reason or another, and especially *lately,* Mark thought, Steve had this terrible habit of rambling and not being able to take a hint. At once he could talk about everything and nothing at all. A man of few words, it was difficult for Mark to understand and sometimes he had this overwhelming feeling to just go over there and clock him. It was hard to explain. In a way Steve had reminded Mark of someone he'd known a long time ago named Lawler, who had been a *dear* childhood friend. He had mentioned that *off-handed* to Cheryl one night. *Well, isn't that a good thing?* Cheryl said. It was and it wasn't, Mark had wanted to explain, but she seemed indifferent and Mark merely shrugged his shoulders.

Nice night we're having, huh? Steve said. I love this weather. Don't you, Mark? Not too warm, not too cold. Good sleeping weather, you know—especially after that summer we had.

Steve, Mark said.

...Sure was hot, Steve said. My God, I couldn't believe how hot it was. I think that air conditioner ran all but two weeks, it was *so* hot. Must be all of that global warming everybody's talking about, he said, and laughed. *Right?*

One of the contractors working at the Clancy house walked over to the white van carrying a ladder with one hand and a bag of tools with the other. He called over to Steve and nodded his head.

Earl, Steve said and gave him a short wave. Steve called for his dog and whistled and started walking over in Mark's direction. He said, Did I ever introduce the two of you? Mark, he said, do you know Earl?

The contractor opened the side door of the van and leaned in, and Steve said, I've known Earl a long time. Me and him *practically* grew up in the trades together. Earl's a great cabinet guy. The best cabinet guy I know, in fact. Steve said, I recommended him to Kevin and Amy for that kitchen renovation they're doing. And I know Cheryl said you might be looking to do a few things at your house in the spring.

Is that so? Mark said.

Steve nodded his head. He smiled. He drew on his cigarette and exhaled. He said, We're always the last ones to know, aren't we? Then he turned around and called to his dog again.

So how are things? Steve said. How's life treating you these days, Mark? And Cheryl? How are things with Cheryl? Anything new to report?

Like what? Mark said. He took his hands from the trash can and stood straight up. He brushed his hands together and then along his trousers.

Steve shrugged his shoulders in no particular way. He flicked the end of his cigarette. I mean, how are things? he said. How's school for Cheryl? How's work? Hey, he said, I saw Cheryl the other night. Both me and Mary did. I don't know if she told you. Did she happen to mention anything—

Beth came to her front door and started calling for her kids. Mark looked over and Steve waved at Beth and Beth turned around and went inside.

Not immediately, but a short time later, Steve said: Damn shame what happened with Tom and Beth, huh? I like those people. Beth, she seems all right, and Tom, I like him. Never a bad word to say about anybody, always pleasant, you know?

Steve licked his lips and reached into his pocket for a handkerchief and blew his nose.

He said, I wasn't home when things happened the other day. Mary was home. She said she heard a lot of screaming, a lot of noise going on—and it wasn't long after the police came.

The contractor nodded his head at Steve again and Steve said, All right, Earl. Earl said something about maybe seeing Steve and his guys at the Foleys next week, and Steve said, All right, Earl. Just let me know. We're ready when you're ready. Then Steve twitched his nose, folded his handkerchief and blew his nose again.

The Party

It's terrible to see something like that happen to two young people, especially when there are *young* kids involved, Steve said. He raised his eyebrows and drew a breath. If they were grown already, maybe it wouldn't be *so* bad; but *hopefully* for the sake of those young kids, they'll figure something out soon...

Earl, the driver of the white van, tooted his horn and pulled away and Cheryl started driving from the opposite direction. Steve stuffed his handkerchief in his back pocket and stood up as tall as possible as Cheryl slowed her little red sports car, *which was gleaming under the last of the day's light.*

She pulled up to the curb and lowered her window just over halfway.

Why hello there, fellas, Cheryl said.

Cheryl, how are you? Steve said.

I'm doing well, Cheryl smiled. Much better than I was doing this morning, thank *you* for asking.

Why hello there, Mark, Cheryl said.

Steve nodded his head and gave Cheryl a big smile. Some night last night, huh? Steve said. He took a few steps closer to that car, closer to where Mark was standing. He could hear the engine of *that* little red sports car humming.

We wanted to come by and see you, Steve said to Cheryl, but it was getting late and Mary needed to get home for work the next morning. He said, I couldn't believe how many people there were. I can't *even* remember the last time I'd seen that many people in one place in my entire life. It was like a *zoo,* he laughed. It was like they were giving something away for free, you know? At one point, I even said it to Mary. I said, 'Mary, be on the lookout for whatever it is they're giving

77

away.' He laughed again. He said, I swear, I don't *even* think we got home until ten or ten thirty. My God, was it late. What a hell of a time we had just getting out of that parking lot, it was so crowded. You should have seen Mary, Steve said. She wasn't a happy camper if you can believe it. *No!* But we were one of the lucky ones. We were one of the first to leave at least. He said, You should have seen that parking lot fill up behind us...

Anyways, I can't *even* imagine what time it was when you got home *yourself.* You must have got home late, he said. *Am I right?* He said, You probably didn't get home until eleven or eleven thirty, *I bet.*

Oh, I don't even know, Cheryl said. She rolled her eyes. She said, These days I hardly know whether I'm coming or going. The last twenty-four hours have been such a whirlwind. I know it was late, that's for sure. Mark was in bed already by the time I got home. I don't even think he heard me come in. *Did you, Mark?* she said. Sleeping like a log, no doubt.

She looked at Mark and grinned. A strand of hair fell across her face and she blew at it from the corner of her mouth. Then, Steve noticed, tucked it behind her ivory ears.

Well, like I said: Mary and I tried to stop by and see you but there was this long line outside your door. It must have gone halfway down the hall. By God, I thought. I told Mary, A lot of people waiting *eagerly* to say hello.

Parents waiting to give me the business, I'm sure, Cheryl laughed.

Steve shook his head. I don't know about that, he said. I couldn't imagine *that* being true at all. I'm sure you're one *hell* of a teacher, Cheryl, he said. In my experience you can always tell the *good* teachers from the *bad* teachers, you know?

The Party

Well, isn't that sweet of you? Cheryl said.

Steve blushed and looked at Mark. He said, Annie was *hoping* that she'd have Cheryl this year. We *all* were. But she got put on the *Red* team, instead. *So* Ms. Maley's her English teacher. Do you know her? Steve said. When Mark didn't answer, Steve shrugged his shoulders and said, She's one of those old-timers, you know?

Now Steve, Cheryl said, Ms. Maley's a *very* good English teacher, I'll have you know. A *wonderful* English teacher, in fact. I'm *sure* Annie loves her, Cheryl said.

Well, maybe she does, Steve said, maybe she doesn't. About *that,* I'm not entirely sure. Annie hasn't said all that much. To tell the truth she hasn't said much about anything. At least she hasn't said she hates her anyways. He shrugged his shoulders again and laughed shortly. But you know kids that age. There's time yet for that, I suppose.

Cheryl smiled and Steve's dog ran over growling some. It ran over to Mark and sniffed at his shoes *carefully.* Then it made a couple of passes from the side yard to the front with its hair up along its spine before settling back down by Steve's side.

Steve, how's the puppy? Max? Cheryl said. His name is Max, right?

Max, Steve said, yes. He looked down at the dog and smiled and shook his head. He said, He's a crazy bastard, all right, and cuffed the dog's ears. Always running around from here to there. Less than two months and he damn near thinks he owns the place. *Don't you?*

The dog looked up at Steve. It had big brown eyes. It was panting. Its tongue was hanging out.

What Could We Have Possibly Known About Love Then?

Look at how much *he* loves you, Cheryl said. How *cute* is that? Mark, Cheryl said, is that not the cutest thing you've ever seen?

Cheryl flashed her eyes and Mark looked quickly at the dog. It wasn't a particularly good-looking dog, Mark thought. It wasn't the kind of dog he would have wanted anyway. At one point, Mark knew, they had talked about getting a dog. Maybe a golden retriever, he thought, or one of those German short-haired pointers he'd always wanted. But this dog *here* had a ragged coat and a snout that was too long for its face and seemed to be a mix of three or four or maybe five different types of dogs.

So what do you think? Cheryl said.

About what? Mark said.

About a dog, Cheryl said. We should get a dog. Mark, why don't we get a dog? Can you imagine? Cheryl said. The two of us with a dog, and Steve here. Then *our* dogs could be friends—

Steve looked at Cheryl. Then he looked at Mark and petted the dog's side. He gave it a tap with his knee—the dog's tail going back and forth wildly.

To tell you the truth, Steve said, I never wanted a dog *myself.* The kids wanted it. The kids and Mary. They'd been begging me for years now about getting one, and I fought them tooth and nail. I was dead set against it. We had a dog years ago, a little terrier, before you moved in here—when Jack and Ruth lived in *your* house. The Bensons. You know, the people you bought the house from?

He looked at Cheryl. She was looking at the rearview mirror, *re*applying lipstick.

Anyways, he said, you know how it goes with dogs—the kids are always making promises, the wife. Steve shook his head. He scratched the dog around the jowls. The dog gave him its paw and Steve took it.

But I have to admit it, Steve said. When I'm right, I'm right. But when I'm wrong, I'm wrong...

Sometimes, he said, I come home from work whipped, just whipped, like I've been beaten to hell or something. You know just one of those days and nobody wants to hear nothing, and then you take this dog here—

Besides, Steve said, he keeps those turkeys away. If nothing else, they don't come around here no more, not like they used to at least. They go *right* next door instead, without even skipping a beat. It's amazing really, he said. The whole lot of them. Have you seen it? I don't know if you remember but they used to gather here every night for mass, Steve said. But now, Steve laughed, they shit a storm all over Tony's lawn. I don't know if you've seen it lately but he rakes and rakes and they shit and shit. I think they're just about driving him half-mad.

Poor Tony, Cheryl said. She smiled wide into the rearview mirror, wiped her right forefinger against her teeth and then pushed her lips into each other. I hope we're not going to be picking on Tony again. I like Tony. Cheryl looked at Steve and frowned. She gave him these soft, pouty lips. She said, Whenever I need somebody and Mark's not home, Tony's always willing to help out. In fact, just last week he came over and helped me move those chairs back onto the front porch. And I hardly needed to do anything for him too.

Well, that's Tony, Steve said. That's Tony all right. Would do anything for you, that's the truth. But he's as crazy as they come too. A good guy to know, but a crazy bastard. Steve said, The other day I saw him vacuuming his driveway for *Christ's sake.* Can you imagine? Then he takes a hose. I said,

What Could We Have Possibly Known About Love Then?

Tony, what the hell are you doing? Don't you have something better to do? Why not go and enjoy yourself? Where's Liz? I said. You know?

Steve shook his head and laughed. He reached down and petted his dog again.

A turkey took off for one of the trees behind Bob and Jenny's house and the dog barked at it.

A minute later a car neither of them recognized pulled down the street and made a slow pass around Cheryl's car.

Well, Cheryl said, I better get going. It's been a long day, she yawned, and I have plenty to do still. She looked at herself in the rearview mirror again and fluffed her hair out with both hands.

Steve looked at her hands. They were good delicate hands. How many times before he had imagined those hands gripped firmly around his cock.

Well, it was good seeing you, Steve, Cheryl said. She brought her head to the window and looked out.

It was good seeing you too, Cheryl, Steve said.

Mark, honey, Cheryl said, I picked up dinner. *So* whenever you're ready.

All right, Mark said.

I stopped at *Ming's,* Cheryl said, and got *your* favorites: Chicken and Broccoli, Kung Pao Shrimp, Moo Shu Pork with those little Mandarin pancakes you like so much...

All right, Mark said again. I'll be in in a few minutes. I have to get the mail.

Well, don't be too long, Cheryl said. I don't want your food to get cold. *Besides,* she said, I can't wait to talk with you about my day, about everything I did. We have a lot to talk about, Mark, Cheryl winked. For the party we're having. You know what I mean?

She looked at Mark and tried to smile but her eyes were no longer warm and bright. She reached down for the gear shift and depressed the clutch but was having a tough time putting the car into drive.

Oh, that reminds me, Steve said, before I forget, there's something I wanted to ask you. Cheryl—Steve said and took a step forward in the direction of Cheryl's car. There's something I wanted to talk with you about.

What is it? Cheryl said shortly. *God damn it!* What do you want?

She looked over at Mark, and when he turned away she batted her eyelashes at Steve and watched Steve's face grow more and more blushed.

What is it? she said again.

The dog started whining.

I wanted to ask you about the party, Steve said. Mary and I were talking. We wanted to ask you if there was anything we could do, anything we could bring—

Oh my *God,* Cheryl said. Mark, do you see? Can you believe it? she said. I think the dog is jealous.

Cheryl pulled her little red sports car into the garage and Mark went over to the mailbox and started *anxiously* through the mail.

There were all these fliers, brochures and catalogues. He couldn't believe how many catalogues there were, how many local businesses had already put Cheryl on their radar in the relatively short amount of time they'd lived in CT.

What Could We Have Possibly Known About Love Then?

How long can this go on for? Mark thought. He was thinking about Boston too.

Maybe if he had stayed with Dara, the girl he'd dated before he'd met Cheryl, and had seen it all the way through, things would have been different. She was a beautiful girl after all—perhaps the most beautiful woman he had ever been with. And she was a talented painter to boot. Sure, she had this unnerving habit of waking suddenly in the middle of the night screaming and sometimes crying when they were making love. *But was that so terrible? Was that the worst thing?*

He tossed the catalogues in the trash and started to rifle through the bills. He took the credit card bill and the gas bill, the bill from the telephone company. All of a sudden he remembered this one spring day when he was thirteen or fourteen years old and he was driving along the *Sikorsky Bridge* with his father and mother and a man jumped up on the rails and threatened to jump off.

You see what happens? his father said to him.

Now what kind of thing is that to say? his mother said.

He'd always wanted to go to Spain, Mark thought. Or maybe to India to try and find religion. God knows he could use a little bit of religion in his life. He put his hands together. He wondered if it would be just as easy to try running from the bulls.

Gimpy is what I call him, Steve said out of nowhere. Have you seen it, Mark? You must have seen him. That gimp bird. Over there. On the Clancy lawn right behind you.

He thought about opening the credit card bill right then and there, or better yet just tearing it in half. He took a deep breath and looked down at his hands. He studied the veins that moved up toward his fingers and raised his head and looked out at the horizon. *All along the valley, he could hear some Indian chieftain say, it was like the tall arms of Heaven reaching up to meet the faces of God!*

There, there, Steve said. There, there. Calm down, will you? Just calm down. Nobody's bothering you. Nobody's trying to take what's not theirs. He chuckled to himself and petted his dog's side. Then he smoked his cigarette down to the filter and tossed it onto the street.

I'm surprised, Steve said. I'd never thought he'd make it, you know? Last year when I'd seen him I'd thought someone would have taken him for dinner. I'd thought he'd be a goner for sure.

Steve looked at the turkey's beady eyes and blue head, its tough beard and the bright red feathers along its neck. He watched closely at the way the turkey's body dipped as it set one crooked leg in front of the other, and continued on.

You should have seen how small he was last year. *Just a baby.* And what a hell of a time he had getting around when the weather was fair enough.

Mark turned the bills over in his hand. He leaned forward and stuffed them into his back pocket. What's that? he said. What's that *now?*

Right there, Steve said. Right behind you. Turn around, he said. Turn around and take a good look. Yes, he said. Yes, yes. That's it. That's it, all right.

Tom Jr. ran out to his front yard, grabbed a football and kicked it as far as he could and ran chasing it, and Steve took a step closer and the dog barked. Mark turned around to leave and the turkey pecked at the ground twice and then stopped.

My God, will you look at that! Steve said. *Jesus, God of Heaven.* Mark, are you looking? Mark, do you see what I see?

It lifted its claw. At once the turkey raised its head and shrieked and looked carefully between the three of them.

What Could We Have Possibly Known About Love Then?

That's some bird all right, isn't it? Steve said.

Then it raised its feathers as though it was posing, and then it spread its wings.

…There was a fair moon out that night which seemed to wash over everything.

Steve's wife Mary had come home late from work and was worn out to the bone but had managed somehow to put something together for the four of them to eat.

During dinner Steve tried talking with his son about the high school football team, how things were going with him: *Did he have a good practice and so on? What did his coach say? Did he think he'd start in the game against Amity? Did his coach give him any sort of indication, one way or the other? What about the Giants? How do you think they're going to do this weekend? Do you think they're going to beat Dallas? Do you think Eli's going to have a big game?*

Then he tried talking with his daughter Annie: *How was school today?* he said to her. *Honey, did you do anything interesting? Which books are you reading now? I heard that Ms. Maley's a very good English teacher. I heard you're lucky to have her…*

After Annie and Steve Jr. asked to be excused from the dinner table (within ten minutes of sitting down) and scurried up to their rooms and Mary started to say things—things like: *Who said anything about making homemade pies? I'm not going to be making homemade pies! If that little bitch wants homemade pie so badly, then why doesn't she goddamn make it herself?*—Steve went out to the front porch and reached into his shirt pocket for the pack of cigarettes.

The Party

For months now, ever since Mary's brother Ray had been diagnosed with cancer, he'd been telling himself that *sooner than later* he needed to quit the nasty habit. That indeed he had a reason to grow old. So he did himself a bit of research. He looked into the patch. He purchased a few packs of that nicotine gum.

From where he was standing it was as though he could see the whole neighborhood.

He removed a cigarette from the pack, brought it to his lips and looked across the street at the lights blinking on and off, at what he figured was Cheryl's silhouette dancing past one of the windows. With his eyes wide open he imagined her in that pretty little sundress she wore from time to time with her long brown hair blowing in the wind and wondered if she'd wear that same dress to the party on Saturday.

My God, he thought, *what I would do for just five minutes with that woman!*

He looked down at his hands. He shook his head and lit his cigarette and looked through the cellophane wrap at the picture of his two kids from when they were no more than three or four years old. *Just babies.*

He recalled this one memory he'd kept of his wife Mary all these years from the summer before their senior year at *Barlow,* when the carnival had come to town, before the twins were *even* a blip on the radar.

What a beautiful summer that was, he thought. He and Mary hadn't been dating all that long.

He drew on his cigarette and tried to get it right: the look on Mary's face, the way she used to look, and *maybe* how he used to look too. He remembered his long hair and the way her slight hips went. He remembered begging her all night to go on that Ferris wheel, and how she *just* wouldn't go.

What Could We Have Possibly Known About Love Then?

Two silly kids, he thought. Him always begging, and how it was never the right time. *I don't like heights,* she kept on saying. *I don't like heights. She was one of those good Catholic girls anyways.*

He remembered the look on her face that night they were strapping her in. She was so scared-looking, so young, so innocent. He thought about how her cheeks got all flushed when they started to go all the way around that first time. How her eyes started to tear in the corner and how the whole world seemed to tremble beneath them for a little bit. *Hold me,* she kept on saying. *Hold me.* He remembered the view he had from there. The way she clung to him, her high-pitched shriek just before they started descending.

Son-of-a-bitch, he thought. *That lucky son-of-a-bitch.* He crossed his ankles and put one hand on his hip and shook his head. *He'd always wanted to be a gunslinger.* He thought he'd never felt anything like that in his entire life.

A cool breeze cut across the front yard and stirred at the leaves and Steve brought his shirt collar in closer to his neck and drew on his cigarette again and started to think about the next week and the week after that.

He thought about that conversation he'd had with the guys on Monday. How in 2008, things got slow for a while, he said, times got lean, but then they picked up *eventually,* they always do—

A car started down the street from the old Miller's Farm where Steve had first seen those turkeys when he plumbed that whole development some fifteen or sixteen years ago now and his whole life seemed to be firmly in front of him. He'd made money hand over fist then. That job was a blessing too. *How many days I sat in the office praying the phone would 'finally' ring and then all of a sudden we were running no less than a dozen guys, and still we couldn't keep up...*

You're damned either way, he laughed, *one way or the other, whether you have too much work or there's never enough. There are certain things that some people just don't understand.* He remembered how in seventy-eight when the gypsy moths passed through, his father working seventeen-hour days for months on end only to find himself in the hospital for it. *Foolish, foolish,* his mother said. *But he was one tough bastard—say what you want. He could be ornery as fuck, that's true. But he lived his life, and he never got in anyone's way of living out their own...*

He cleared his throat and hacked up a bit of something. His dog started barking again and he took out his handkerchief and blew his nose and wiped across his lips.

He stood there frozen awhile and thought about that estimate he'd given Dunhill Construction Group for that big addition over on North Adams Road (for the president of Remington-Pace), and, if everything went the way it was supposed to, *possibly* for some work on the guest house too.

"Is that the best you can do?" Jack Dunhill said.

Maybe we could have shaved off a few hundred after all...

He didn't leave much room for error, he knew that. He'd hardly accounted for material and labor as it was.

Steve drew on his cigarette again and he felt the slow burn against his fingers and tried looking well enough down the road, well past Sam and Cathy Myers' house and Al Baker and his wife, where there were just trees and grass and no lights at all.

At once he thought about Paul Newman in *The Left Handed Gun.* Deke Thornton and Pike Bishop and Elizabeth Taylor in *Cat on a Hot Tin Roof.*

What Could We Have Possibly Known About Love Then?

"Let's go!" he said. "Why not?!" he said.

He thought about his father and the last time he'd seen him. He thought about *Angel* and *Joe Buck* too. He laughed a moment and shook his head.

There was a rustle in one of the trees behind Tony's house and Steve looked over in its direction and smiled to himself.

Gimpy, he said. Tough little guy.

He blew out a big puff of smoke and finished his cigarette and went into his shirt pocket and reached for another.

"And you know what you can do with them dishes and cups and things, *don't you?!* And if you're just some *chicken-little,* well, shoot, I'd be more than happy to oblige…"

He turned around and looked at himself in the mirror. He struck his match and fired one shot, then the other.

"Oh my God, Joe, it's you. It's really you, isn't it? You, you're the only one."

Not long after, his dog came running over and he bent down slowly and petted it.

The Storm

There was a storm coming on. He could feel it in his bones. The day had been bright and sunny and the vast blue sky seemed to trail on forever, but all morning, he knew, the temperatures had been dropping steadily, the birds from their rock perches set high upon the cliff had been flying low over the water line, and although the leaves barely stirred from the long reaches of the towering pin oaks and seasoned maples that had taken root all around that particular stretch of the shoreline, there was the recognizable smell of the great winds turning at the ocean floor.

Just beyond the dunes and the tall grasses, the hedges of wild rose and beach plum and cherry blossom and elder, children built sandcastles with towers and giant motes and ran along the beach laughing under the watchful eyes of their parents as young couples walked hand-in-hand westward along the shore in the direction of the old wooden pier where fathers and their sons fished for bass and cod and bluefish and flounder and a growing mass of eager-eyed surfers began to suit up and wax their boards while talking energetically about tomorrow and the days after tomorrow.

Usually around this time of year the storms tended to blow eastward and follow the track of the warmer air out to sea, but earlier in the week, a few hundred miles off the coast of

Florida, the storm took a decided turn westward toward the mainland and seemed to be gathering strength as it held a steady course for New England.

If this had been any other time the last thirty years—just a year back *even,* before Sam Hardy retired and his son *officially* took over the business—Janie Hardy would have joked to family and friends that her husband Sam had been out all night dancing, shouting from the rooftops, chanting his ancient Indian rain songs.

A kind and soft-spoken religious man who was never looking to benefit from someone else's misfortune, certainly even Sam would have admitted how the storms and the natural catastrophes which had befallen the otherwise quiet New England town the last thirty years or so had been a blessing for him and his family as he had built his landscaping business on the backs of the gypsy moths which had torn through in the late seventies, for instance, and the havoc wreaked by Hurricane Gloria in 1985. By the time the shoreline got pummeled six years later by Bob and then Irene, Sam had grown his business to more than thirty full-time employees, had put all three of his children through private high school and then college and had saved enough money to buy the old McKinley house at the Point with the large wrap-around porch and the old widow's peak, from where, it was said, Mrs. McKinley would sit all night, year after year, staring out at the ocean and the glittering lights from the beacon and the stars above, waiting for Mr. McKinley and the other men to come home.

It was Janie who had told that story best. Her grandmother had told it to her so many times when she was a little kid that it had worn a special place in her heart. They were married more than sixty years, she'd say, and they loved each other so, and each time Mr. McKinley was away, Mrs. McKinley would turn on every single light in that house so that by nightfall it was like a thousand lamps burning in a sea of darkness.

Sam reached his hands into the gutter, cleared out the last of the debris and shook out his hands and looked at them. The sun was high and his hands were golden brown and powerful-looking under the light, and he looked carefully at the half-moons and at the veins while he searched above the ladder, measured the pitch of the roof with his eyes and considered the rain from the storm rushing into the gutters, pouring into the downspouts and settling into the earth.

They were strong hands *still,* he told himself. Powerful hands *still* capable of building a great many things, he thought. Or running a saw if he had to during the height of the storm with his left foot steady upon the fallen limb, the smoke from his cigar mixing with the heat from the motor and smell of the wood as he edged the blade further into the limb, guiding it mostly *to just about the breaking point,* but not pushing it, and never forcing it as his father had shown him and as he in turn had shown his own son.

As Sam descended the ladder, at the beach one of the lifeguards stood upon the chair and whistled and waved at a group of young boys swimming near the rocks about forty yards out, and with one hand held up to the high afternoon sun, Sam turned and narrowed his eyes to see if it was the Johnson boy *again* or maybe the Kelly boy who was causing all that commotion.

He's going to make me an old woman soon enough. He's going to be the end of me, that's for sure, Mrs. Johnson said the last time Sam had seen her in town.

But they were good-natured boys, Sam thought. They were harmless overall. Maybe a little dim-witted through the ears,

Sam laughed. But they'll come around. Boys like that, they always do.

He picked up his ladder and carried it to the side of the garage. Then he collected all of the tools he used that morning to secure the storm windows and to clean out the gutters, and he carefully put them away.

Sam, there's a world of difference between doing a job and doing it correctly, he could hear his father say as he carried the five-gallon bucket of debris to the compost pile, emptied it, washed the bucket out and hung it upside down on a fence post to dry.

He looked down at his watch. It was a quarter to one. He would have liked to have gone to the end of the pier to see if any of the young boys or the old man had caught the big fish that had been spotted a couple of weeks back, but he didn't think he had enough time. At the very least, he figured, it would take him about fifteen minutes to walk the length of the beach to the end of the pier, and once he got there he knew he was never in much of a hurry to leave.

The kitchen smelled of flowers and of the summer when Sam walked in. Janie was at the kitchen table writing and for a brief moment Sam glanced around at the gleaming countertops and the white tiled floor and the vases of fresh-cut flowers on nearly every surface.

As he went over to the sink he noticed the cutting board and the sharp electric knife along with the colander and large roasting pan awaiting the dinner Janie had planned on cooking them for their anniversary later that evening.

The Storm

Thirty-nine years, Sam thought as a breeze cut through the house and Janie clutched at the top of her collar. Next year it would have been forty.

Sam walked over to the cupboard and reached for a glass and turned on the kitchen faucet and poured himself a glass of water.

How is it out there? Janie said without looking up. Is it warm? It feels like it's getting cooler out.

It's warm, Sam said. It's getting cooler too, but it's still warm, he said, especially with the sun out.

Janie lifted her head momentarily and winked at Sam, who smiled and drank his water.

Did you see anybody? Was anybody down at the beach? Janie asked.

The Bradys are there, Sam said. I saw Ed Pickney and his wife too, and their grandkids.

Oh, how are they doing? Janie said. Did you talk to them?

Good, Sam said. Everybody's good. They were asking for you. They wanted to know how you were doing, how everybody was getting along.

And what did you say? she said, again without looking up.

I said everybody's fine. I said maybe you'd go down and say hello if you had the chance later.

I'd like to do that, Janie said. If I could find the time I'd like to do it.

You should try, Sam nodded his head.

Maybe I will, Janie said.

Sam ran the back of his right hand along his forehead and wiped the beads of sweat onto his trousers. Then he drank the rest of his water and turned on the faucet and filled his glass again and drank another mouthful.

What Could We Have Possibly Known About Love Then?

Janie said, Michael called a little while ago when you were up on the ladder putting in the storm windows and said if you needed him at all he'd stop by.

And what did you say? I hope you didn't tell him I needed him.

I wouldn't dare, Janie said. I said, You know your father, as long as he can manage he doesn't want anyone meddling in his business.

He has a lot to do himself, you know, Sam said.

I know it, Janie said.

Sam turned the glass in his hand and looked at Janie, who had her head down still and was writing.

And what did he say to that? Sam said.

He said you were stubborn, of course. Why is he breaking his back, climbing up and down those ladders when he could just send over a couple of guys? I said, Michael, you don't even know the half of it. I said, Michael, whatever you think about your father being stubborn or otherwise, multiply it by ten, if not twenty.

Is that right? Sam said.

That's right, Janie shook her head and laughed.

Sam drank the rest of his water and looked at the clock as Janie coughed and laughed again, shuddering while she drew her robe quickly up against her neck.

Where is Michael now? He must be at the shop.

I think he was going to meet Billy and some of the other guys, Janie said.

To get the saws ready, I'm sure, Sam said, and to load up the trucks—

Janie folded the piece of stationary into thirds. She stuffed the stationary into an envelope and began licking the flap.

I hate that taste, you know?

The glue, you mean?

Janie looked at Sam and made a sour face. Then she licked her lips and blinked her eyes. She pressed the flap down and used a piece of Scotch tape and turned the letter over and opened her address book.

What are you doing? Sam said to her.

I was just writing a letter to my cousin Rose, Janie said.

How come? Sam said.

I don't know, Janie said. I guess I just got to thinking about how close we'd all been at one time before she and Jim moved out to California, you know, and how crazy it is that we haven't talked to each other in a while. So I figured I'd write her a quick letter while I had the time, and I figured you could mail it for me when you went into town if that's all right. You don't mind, do you?

No, I don't mind. It's right there. I can do it.

And I think you're going to need a stamp too. I think we ran out of stamps. Janie said, I looked all over the place but I couldn't find any, so you might want to get a whole book when you're down there.

All right, Sam said.

Which reminds me, Janie said. She took her time and wrote down the address *neatly,* closed the address book and handed the envelope to Sam. Then she took the sheet of paper marked "For Sam" that had been under her notebook of recipes and looked over what she'd already written and added "stamps" to it.

Here, she said to him.

What's this?

She handed him the piece of paper and he ran his hands through his beard.

It's the list of things I want you to get when you go into town, Janie said. Most of the things we've talked about already, but then I added a couple of things too along the way. For instance, I thought you might want to pick up some batteries, she said, and maybe an extra box of candles just in case. And then, she said, I thought it might be good for you to have a few extra gallons of water and some bread and crackers and cans of tuna and soup or whatever you think you might be in the mood for—

I think it's probably too warm for soup, you know, Sam said. I'm not sure I'm going to pick up any soup.

Well, it's up to you, Janie said. Whatever you want. Nothing's set in concrete. It's just a suggestion, you know. But if change your mind I saw in the circular that they're having a sale on that Mrs. Greens soup you love. You know, the beef barely. So if you want to pick up a couple of cans, you never know. Besides it's not like it goes bad.

All right, Sam said.

But like I said it's up to you.

Okay.

And then you were talking about getting your haircut, weren't you?

I was thinking about it.

That's what you said, isn't it?

Sam nodded his head and then he ran his hands through his beard again.

Which reminds me, Janie said. You're never going to guess what I found when I was going through the things in the attic. Wait until you see this, she said. You want to laugh. She said, I want you to take this with you and show it to Nicky when you see him and see what he says. I'm sure he'll get a big kick out of it too.

What is it? Sam said, glancing up at Janie momentarily before going back to the list.

Remember that girl he used to go with from Ludlowe...? Janie said.

Sam thought about it. But he could not remember specifically because Nick had a lot of girls back then. They all did.

Well, wait. You just wait.

Janie picked up the address book and put it down. Then she grabbed the stationary pad and put that down. Now where did I put it? Janie said. She pushed herself up slowly, looking all around her at all the papers on the table.

You know, I could just stay here, Sam interjected. I could stay here and help you.

Don't be silly, Janie shook her head and coughed. She drew a deep breath and leaned over and coughed again.

We've talked about this, she said, smiling. You promised me. Besides the last thing I want to do while I'm trying to cook us a special dinner is to have you around here interfering, asking me a million questions and putting your oar in everything.

I wouldn't do that, Sam said.

Like hell you wouldn't, Sam Hardy, Janie laughed. Besides, she said to him, when was the last time you got your haircut? She put her hands on her hips and looked at him squarely.

I don't know, Sam said. Six weeks. Maybe a couple of months.

What Could We Have Possibly Known About Love Then?

Exactly, Janie said and winked. Now I need you to get all of the things on that list, she said. And don't you think it'll be nice to see you all cleaned up.

Being that it was summer there was plenty of traffic all along the main road through town and not surprisingly it took Sam a few hours to run from Rikener's Pharmacy to Mrs. Greens out to Henderson's Hardware then over to the post office to mail the letter Janie had written her cousin Rose, along with a package she'd put together for Mary, their daughter, who lived in North Carolina with her husband Paul and had two children of her own.

At Jim Webber's place Sam ran into Fred Avery, an old hunting buddy who in just a few short minutes had already loaded his cart with six boxes of shells, field wipes, two cans of cover scent, a new pair of gloves, a half dozen tube socks and a hundred feet of nylon rope, et cetera, et cetera, for a trip he and Joe Williams were planning to take up north at the end of the month.

You should come with us, Fred said right away as he and Sam looked over the fishing poles and the reels and began poring over the extensive selection of jigs. Maybe bring your son, Fred added. Joe Williams was planning on bringing his sons. And I think one of the grandkids is going too.

We'll see, Sam said.

I mean it, Fred Avery said. It should be a real good time. When was the last time the three of us did anything together? Besides you must be driving Janie up a wall now that you're retired and have all that time on your hands, and I bet a dollar to donuts she'd be looking to get rid of you for the week, am I right?

You might be, Sam said. I wouldn't doubt it.

You better believe it, Fred Avery smiled as Sam picked up a spincast reel and set it back down, then grabbed a baitcasting reel which was the same type his father always used and began turning it over in his hand.

Watching carefully, Fred Avery said, Hey Sam, has anyone caught that monster fish the old man swore he saw swimming around the pier?

What's that? Sam said.

…Anyways, you should really think about it, Fred Avery concluded a few minutes later. It's going to be a hell of a good time. Might be good to get away, you know. Hey Sam, have you been doing a lot of hunting lately?

The barber shop was quiet when Sam walked in. A few chairs down from the door a man was sitting next to a little girl in a yellow dress. The man's hair looked freshly trimmed, Sam noted, and the little girl with blonde pigtails had a picture book on her lap and was sucking on a lollipop. In the barber's chair sat a little boy, who had dark hair and dark eyes just like the man.

Hey Sam, Nick said when Sam walked in.

Nick, Sam said.

The man on the side of the little girl looked up at Sam and nodded his head and Sam looked at the man and the little girl and smiled.

How is it outside? Nick, the barber, said.

It's all right, Nick, Sam said.

Have the winds started yet?

Not so much yet.

Maybe we'll get lucky then, Nick said. What do you think?

Maybe, Sam said. You never know.

Nick peered at Sam over the tops of his wire-rimmed glasses and Sam walked over to the magazine rack, grabbed the latest copy of *Outdoor Magazine* and took the open seat to the left of the little girl, who, when he sat down was chuckling to herself, inspecting her lollipop and kicking her feet gleefully back and forth.

On the cover of the magazine a young father and a little boy waded out in a stream with their lines cast, and as he settled into his chair, crossing one leg over the other and then leaning back, Sam studied the current and the small shadows that were beginning to form on the young man's face as he tried to decide what time of day it was and how much longer the man and the little boy would have until night fell and (probably because the mother would want them home before it got too late) they'd have to turn in.

I was just telling Dave about the storm that blew through in ninety-eight, Nick said all of a sudden, when they had to helicopter old Mr. Wilson and his wife from their house on Reef Road because they were too stubborn to leave.

That was some storm, Sam said.

Do you remember? Nick said.

I remember, all right, Sam said, nodding affirmatively and then glancing at the man to the right of the little girl who, he noticed, was looking between the two of them smiling.

Nobody was going to tell Tim Wilson what to do, Nick laughed. Not even the police, do you remember? Even when the police tried to take him out the day before, he told them it was his house after all, his life, and if he'd seen one storm, well, he'd seen them all. Nick laughed again. He took the boy's hair between his two fingers and cut straight across. But then, of course, the rains came and the waters flooded over from the creek in the back and he changed his tune quick all right, old Mr. Wilson did.

He sure did, Sam said. He really didn't have a choice.

Not unless he wanted to go for a long swim, Nick said.

He combed through the boy's hair carefully. Then he turned the barber's chair ninety degrees and changed scissors.

But I don't think it's going to be anything like that. I don't think it'll be nearly as bad.

No, Sam said. I don't think so.

Nick peered over the tops of his glasses at the two men, and the boy turned to look at himself in the mirror. Then the phone rang and Nick walked over to answer it. Sam shifted in his chair and began turning the pages of his magazine. "White Hills Barber Shop," Nick called out.

Sam was looking at a photograph of an enormous buck with giant antlers on a hill overlooking a valley when out of the corner of his eye he noticed the little girl looking up at him with her head bent inquisitively as though, he thought to himself, he too was like that old buck in the woods.

He began looking at his hands. Clenching his fingers to form a fist, but mostly wiggling his fingers back and forth as though he were preparing to play the piano.

Mommy said we don't have to go to school tomorrow, the girl began kicking her feet back and forth excitedly. Still looking at him, she said, *Mommy* said we don't have to go to school tomorrow or the next day or the day after that...

Is that so? Sam said, letting his hands drop.

Maybe not for a whole week, the little girl said. Maybe not ever.

Do you have school? I didn't think little girls went to school in the middle of the summer, Sam said.

The man looked at Sam and smiled and Nick hung up the phone and turned back to the little boy, who was still looking at himself in the mirror.

Mommy said we're going to play board games and eat ice cream and make tents and have pancakes with syrup, the little girl said.

Is that so? Sam said.

The little girl looked at Sam and nodded her head. Then she looked down at the book in her lap and swung her legs. Mommy said we're going to bake a cake.

Well, well, Sam said, aren't you lucky?

The little girl nodded her head.

And what kind of cake are you going to bake? My favorite is chocolate. Do you like chocolate cake?

The little girl was nodding her head still, but then she turned back to her father questioning, and began shaking her head from side to side.

So you *don't* like chocolate cake? Sam said.

The girl shook her head again and laughed. Then she brought her hands to her face and laughed again. I like vanilla, she said.

Oh, vanilla, Sam said.

The girl nodded her head.

My wife likes vanilla cake too, Sam said. In fact, vanilla cake is her favorite, he said. Vanilla cake with whipped cream and strawberries. Do you like vanilla cake with whipped cream and strawberries?

The little girl took her hands and pressed them against her eyes, and then spread her fingers to look through them. Then she laughed and moved the lollipop in her mouth with her left hand and showed two fingers with her right hand.

Two? Sam said.

No, the little girl said. She looked at her hand and added another finger. *Three!* the little girl shouted excitedly.

Oh, three, Sam said.

The little girl nodded her head, and Sam said, What does that mean, *three?* Are you planning on baking *three* cakes?

The little girl looked at him slightly confused. Sam laughed, and the little girl said, No, *I'm* three.

Oh, *you're* three, Sam said.

The little girl nodded her head. I'm three and a half, she said and swung her legs back and forth.

Oh, you're three and a *half,* Sam said to her.

And then next year I'll be four, and then I'll be five, and then I'll be six, and then I'll be seven…

Do you want to guess how old I am? Sam said to her at once.

The little girl nodded her head. Then she turned the lollipop in her mouth. Sam held up all ten of his fingers, but then he quickly took the left pinky away and the little girl looked at him strangely. Then she tilted her head to the side and took the lollipop out of her mouth and looked at that too. Then she looked at her father and then at her shoes. She put the lollipop back in her mouth and turned back to her book and swung her legs back and forth and began flipping the pages.

Well, Dad, what do you think? Nick said to the father. He turned the chair around and made one or two minor adjustments as the young father stood and the little boy stared straight ahead and the young father took a few steps over.

I think it looks good, the young father said.

What Could We Have Possibly Known About Love Then?

And what do you think, young man? Nick took a brush to the back of the boy's neck and went around with his comb. Naturally, the boy did not say anything and the father walked over to the cash register and the girl got up and Nick grabbed the fishbowl of lollipops and held them out in front of the little boy, who took a green one and then looked at Nick *closely* to see if he could take another.

When the door swung closed, Nick went over to the corner with the red and brown horse chair the little boy had been sitting on, lowered the shades, locked the door and turned the sign at the window from open to closed.

Sam went over to the magazine rack, and Nick peered over the tops of his glasses quickly, glancing around the room, and called: Next gentleman!

I guess I'm the last customer, Nick?

That's it, Nick said. Last customer.

He did a quick but thorough sweep of the floor, and then he grabbed the tissue paper that was around the boy's neck and tossed it into the garbage.

So what are we going to do today? Nick said. The *usual?*

He peered over the tops of his glasses at Sam's thick beautiful hair. Then he shook out the apron and fitted it carefully with the pins around Sam's neck. He combed his fingers instructively through the sides and along the top. Take a little bit off the side, keep it longer in the back, trim up the beard.

I don't know, Sam said.

Sam ran his hands through his beard and looked at himself in the mirror. Nick peered at Sam over the tops of his glasses. Then the phone rang and Nick turned around.

I was thinking about shaving the beard off completely.

Not *trimming,* Nick said, but *shaving?*

106

That's right, Sam said. He ran his hands along his beard again while Nick looked at him inquisitively, and said, I thought maybe I'd surprise Janie. She's been after me a long time to shave off this beard, and I thought, well hell, maybe it's time. I want to surprise her, you know.

I think she'll be surprised all right. When was the last time you were clean shaven, high school?

The phone kept ringing. But Sam stared straight ahead into the mirror, and then shifted in his chair. Meanwhile, Nick walked back around with his scissors, and then stood there watching.

I wonder if she'll recognize me, Sam said. Then: Yes, I'm sure. I think she'll get a big kick out of it, all right.

He kept the windows down and took the long way home. Up ahead a line of slow-moving clouds were beginning to form, and Sam ran his fingers *curiously* along his face, feeling the cleanly shaven skin, looking up at the rearview mirror every now and again as he continued down Sherman, took a right onto Puritan, another right onto Harbor and followed the waterline all the way down past the two churches and the grammar school and the old library with the bunny fountain out front from when he was just a kid.

Turning left onto Pequot Avenue he could see the traffic lights ahead (leading all the way down the main street) and for a moment he squeezed the wheel and considered seeing his son to make sure the saws were indeed ready and the wheels on the chippers properly greased. Along with the customer cards in the office already lined up and set to go. He might need me, he said aloud, and I won't be long. But then he remembered what his son had said about loosening up on the reigns at one point, and how he had put his time in and now it was his son's turn. It's all right, Dad, his son had assured him afterward when they eventually sat down to talk about the results. You go home and take care of mom. It's okay, Dad. I'll take care of everything here.

When he walked through the front door Janie was stretched out on the sofa in the family room sleeping. The radio was playing softly as a good breeze pushed through the open windows sending the freshly laundered curtains back and forth, mixing together the smell of the flowers everywhere and the chicken and potatoes coming from the kitchen and the lingering smell of the old liniments and oils that had seemed to burrow themselves in the wood yet all these weeks later. Nearly a month after Janie had first told Sam about her plan and then made him agree to help her clean up the place, and to restore the old McKinley house to its proper grandeur. So that if her grandmother or anyone else for that matter ever came back a hundred years from now, she'd be able to recognize it and know down deep in her heart that they had been good stewards of the place.

And so he helped her to get rid of the bed which for the last six months had become a fixture in the family room, along with the pile of blankets, and the sixteen different types of medication and boxes of tissues everywhere and the buckets she alternated between on those long dark nights when she didn't have the strength to get out of bed.

Janie looked so comfortable lying there in her robe beneath the two layers of blankets that Sam wondered if he should wake her. What if she slept through the night? he thought. What if I just let her sleep? But they'd talked this out a hundred times before, if not close to a thousand, and he knew how upset she'd be if he didn't wake her as soon as he got home so they'd have as much time as possible to sit out on the front porch and enjoy a wonderful dinner together (a feast, a grand feast, she said) before the storm came through and they would have to fall back inside.

Sam took a deep breath and moved closer and the screen door pulled away from its latch and Janie rolled upon her neck slowly and like a child, Sam thought, began to open her eyes.

Is that you? Janie said yawning. Sam, *honey,* is that you?

Yes, it's me, Janie, Sam said. It's me. I'm right here.

What time is it, honey? Janie yawned.

It's almost five, sweetie.

Oh God! Janie went to push herself up—She was blinking her eyes slowly open and closed still with hardly the strength to make it all the way around—and Sam went over to her and knelt down.

Did you just get home? I didn't even hear you walk in.

You looked so comfortable, Sam explained. I didn't want to wake you.

I *was* comfortable, Janie yawned. She went to remove the blankets and tried to swing her legs to the floor. I had the most incredible dream.

Here, let me help you, Sam said. Here, he said. He leaned in closer as she opened her eyes and he put one hand under her arm and the other by her hips.

It was really a wonderful dream—

Are you ready? he said to her. Careful now, he said as he helped her to her feet, holding onto her hips to steady her as she bent over to cough a couple of times to loosen the phlegm that had been building in her chest.

How do you feel?

109

I'm all right.

Good, good.

I'm okay.

Sure you are.

Yes, she said.

So you had a beautiful dream?

Sam rubbed her back gently and Janie reached into her robe pocket for more Kleenex.

I did, honey. I really did.

What was the dream about? he said to her.

All sorts of things. Do you *really* want to know?

Sure I do. He helped her to stand up straight. Tell me.

But it was rather silly.

No, he said to her. No. Tell me. I really want to know.

Oh, honey, she said. But just as she started, it was then, right then, that she saw his face. His face, she thought. For the first time in all these years...

My God, I almost forgot what you looked like, Janie said. She took her cold thin bony hands along his cheekbones and across his chin.

Look at you, she said. Then: My God, for a moment I hardly recognized either one of us.

I thought I'd surprise you, Sam said right away. It's still a bit raw, you know. But in another couple of hours, Nick said, the swelling should go down.

Sam laughed uncomfortably as his wife's eyes narrowed and a sudden breeze came in.

So what do you think, Janie? Sam said. What do you think about what I'd done here?

Oh, honey, she gasped. My God, sweetie, she gasped. Look at you. Look at you. Look at what a young and beautiful and handsome man you are!

110

The Storm

That night they had a wonderful dinner of chicken and potatoes and string beans, a large salad and pasta and homemade bread and a vanilla layered cake for dessert.

After dinner Janie cleared the plates and washed them and put everything away, and then they sat there on the front porch awhile talking and laughing and listening to the radio as the wind picked up and started to blow more aggressively at the trees.

At one point when they were talking about the storm and Janie asked Sam if he'd gotten everything in town that he needed, Sam thought he was going to get sick but then Janie reached for his hand and squeezed it and told him how much she loved him and asked him to put another log on the fire.

Go ahead, Sam. It's starting to die down, and don't you dare get soft on me now.

He looked at her desperately. Are you cold?

I'm all right, she said. Don't worry about me. I'm okay, she pressed. I'm just fine.

So he walked across the porch to the fire pit and knelt down. He removed the screen and added another log to the fire while Janie strained herself with every bit of effort to stand, leaning over at one point to cough to loosen the phlegm.

Now you just wait right here, Janie said. Wait right here. I'll be right back.

Where are you going? Sam said. He turned the log over and then set the poker down. The fire crackled and he walked back over to help, but Janie clutched her robe tight about her and shook, No, no. That's all right. You just stay here, sweetie, and make sure the fire is nice and strong, and let me go inside and get ready.

What Could We Have Possibly Known About Love Then?

But maybe I should come along. Let me help you. I can help, he said. Whatever you need me to do.

But she shook her head again even as he moved closer.

Why not? He reached for her hand, but she pushed away.

Because there's something I want to show you, she said smiling. I have a surprise for you too. Now you stay here. I mean it. You promised. You're not the only one, you know.

And twenty minutes later (as Janie made her way down the stairs and across the family room to the outside), Sam stood at the edge of the porch listening to the sound of the leaves blowing against the crackle of the fire as he moved his hands in and out, rubbing the two of them firmly together, blowing on them, trying to remember how it was just a year before when he was still at work and Janie had not gotten dizzy all of a sudden and fallen and his hands were calloused still and strong as he leaned his left leg into the felled trunk of the old Thomas maple tree and eased the long blade of the saw through, careful not to force it too quick.

In the distance just beyond the immediate upstart of wind and the thrashing of the trees Sam could hear the surprising sound of a plane going overhead and then what sounded like a young man's voice calling out to someone down by the pier, and he suddenly recalled the young doctor in the small office who *nervously* pointed ahead to the dark spots on the X-rays where, he said, there should be all light, and then the look on Janie's face as the doctor began to explain how the cancer had settled deep into her bones already and had worked its way along her spine up to the brain—

How brave she had been then. It was startling really. The whole time he had known her, he thought, more than forty years, she had never faltered, not once, not even once, and though he had been afraid, he had been quite afraid, now he knew exactly what he needed to do.

So he kept his back to the screen door and closed his eyes just as she requested, and he listened carefully as she pushed the door open and coughed and made her way slowly across the porch.

Don't look! Janie said. *Don't look!* You promised me you wouldn't look. Now keep your eyes closed. There's something I want to show you.

All right, he said to her.

I mean it, she said.

It's okay, Janie.

Can I trust you? she said.

And of course he didn't have to think about it. Not at all.

You look beautiful, he said instantly.

Do you really think so? she said.

It had taken her a couple of minutes but eventually she turned him around slowly and uncovered his eyes, swinging her hips from side to side the best she could, smiling as her frail body shivered in the cold.

She said, You would have figured it'd be moth-eaten by now, wouldn't you? Being in the attic for as long as it had been. But look at it, she said. Look at it closely. In a way it's like it's brand new, don't you think, and how many women my age can *still* fit in their high school prom dress?

She said, Do you remember what I said to you when you came up to me?

He was looking at her. He really was. For the first time in a long time, he knew. Though he had always loved her.

He nodded his head.

Well, she said.

113

I'm waiting, he smiled. Go ahead. It's your turn.

And he stood there staring at her, loving her, as she dipped her head and smiled and the fire crackled and the wind blew at the trees.

You're one of those Hardy boys, aren't you? Janie seemed to say all at once, looking away and pretending to be not all that interested.

I'm Sam, he said. Sam Hardy.

Well, Sam, Sam Hardy, she said, and leaned over and coughed and then looked back up at him.

What's the point of staring at someone all night if you're not going to ask a girl to dance?

The next morning the storm came through. And twenty-four hours later, the sun rose and a giant rainbow trailed across the vast blue sky as the people came out and combed the beaches and the local neighborhoods to assess the damage.

When asked, the neighbors would later tell the police that maybe what they'd heard were two gun shots within minutes of each other but understandably of course they couldn't be sure. They knew the old woman had been sick for some time now, they said, and looking back one could say that for more than a month the old man went around every square inch of that house as though he might have been making plans himself. But they were such a regular old couple after all, and who could have fathomed something like this happening in your own backyard. Plus, when questioned, the woman two houses down, who was new to the area herself, said all night she had been thinking about something else. Her husband and kids had gone to bed and she sat on her deck with a bottle of wine, listening to the sound of the trees tossing back and forth and the horrible sound the wind made.

Unexpectedly, it no longer seemed important. Which is the reason why the ten-piece band (in the old love story) is instructed to play as the ship goes down with no clear hope in sight for more than a thousand miles in all directions. Which is the same reason why it is impossible to serve two masters. Or insist that God be placed on a mantle that is too high for what it means to be compassionately human. The sun persists as we make our way each morning in the dark room, which we call a body, and search around for the heart. A song which is contingent upon the morning light, and is not.

An Old Love Story

The Two of Us Like That, You Know

One night Maureen and I were sleeping when we woke up suddenly. First, Maureen woke up. I'd find out later she'd been up for some time. And then I woke up. I was in the midst of a deep sleep, a heavy dream, when she started hitting me across the chest. That's when I shot right up. All of a sudden it'd felt like someone was beating the hell out of me.

Jack! Maureen said. Jack!

What is it? I said. What's wrong?

You don't hear that? Tell me you don't hear that!

Hear what?

That noise!

What noise?

I reached toward the nightstand and turned the lamp on. Then I fumbled for my glasses and put those on. I turned back toward Maureen who was lying there, staring up at the ceiling with the comforter pulled tight around her neck, mumbling something about fire, about guns, (perhaps machetes! she said), about maybe taking a container of lighter fluid and tossing a series of grenades.

I pushed my glasses to the top of my forehead and rubbed my eyes. I yawned and licked my lips. Maureen had wrenched all of the blankets to her side of the bed and my feet were sticking out. So I reached behind me for what I could.

What Could We Have Possibly Known About Love Then?

Then I closed my eyes and I took a deep breath. I brought my hands to my chest and my thoughts started to drift, my arms started to go numb, my legs started to tingle.

...All of a sudden everything went grainy and I found myself on an ancient fishing vessel with a hundred-foot mast and a man dressed in a long white doctor's coat who had introduced himself to me previously as the captain. You don't look like a captain, I said. Is that so? the man said. He had a giant beard and long flowing hair that ran well past his shoulders. I was eating a tuna fish sandwich at the time and the captain began to polish his glass eye as though he were a tall, thin handsomely-mustached waiter polishing a heavy water goblet at a very expensive French bistro. My stomach was growling uncontrollably. I can't believe how hungry I am, I said. It's the only way I can see clearly, the captain responded. I looked up at the masses of long-winged birds with giant beaks and long talons circling overhead and I bit into my tuna sandwich and mayonnaise dribbled all the way down my chin. It was all over my hands too. God damn it! I said. But the captain merely laughed. I was noticeably upset but he was busy waxing his eye. C'mon, I heard him say. You have to admit that it's pretty funny after all.

...Of course it had been my intention to confide in the captain about a "very important" meeting I was scheduled to have with the President and other high-ranking government officials later that day. But as if to cut me off at the pass, I thought. Or to screw with me! Or perhaps as a way of suggesting something more, out of the blue what appeared to be a slightly overweight but otherwise happy hairless orangutan broke through the fog, circling the boat with one of the most graceful breaststrokes I had ever seen. Son of a bitch! I said aloud. It's pretty ironic, isn't it? was the captain's reply.

The Two of Us Like That, You Know

I was looking around for a napkin. But finding none I started licking my hands. There should be buckets of rain around here somewhere, the captain offered. But really all I want to do is go back to sleep, I said, because when I was younger I got thrown off a horse.

...The captain poured three brandies and produced a fistful of exotic Cuban cigars as the orangutan climbed aboard and started to play Petrushka *on the violin. I nodded my head and the captain looked at me through his glass eye. What kind of horse was it? A great Dane, I said. Is that so? The captain took a step back. We started talking in hushed tones. He invited me to sit down. Just ahead in the immediate distance I could see a tiny island approaching with what sounded like tribesmen gathering at the apex of a tall mountain with giant plumes of smoke. I was wearing high heels at the time and hoped the captain wouldn't notice. I hope we're not going there? I said visibly shaken. Don't tell me you're afraid? What if it erupts? I said. Isn't that the plan?*

I'm getting sick and tired of it! I can't take it anymore! I mean who the hell do these people think they are to go on all night long with this shit? Some of us have to work in the morning, you know! Some of us can't just sleep all day! I mean tell me you don't hear that, Jack! Jack, Maureen screamed, tell me I'm the only one!

I wiped my hands across my eyes and yawned. I dangled my legs almost all the way down to the floor and rolled across my back. Why don't you just try to ignore it? I said. It's all right. Maureen, just try to go back to sleep. I turned back over and buried my face in the pillow. My feet were cold and I rubbed them together, and then I thought about getting socks.

But Maureen laughed loudly and started flailing her legs. Honey, I said. Don't honey me! she said. Can you hear this? I started to drift! Am I going crazy? Is this really happening? Am I losing my mind?

…The waters had started to build up. Out of nowhere there were forty-foot swells and now masses upon masses of giant birds circling everywhere. I didn't necessarily trust the orangutan who was constructing a helicopter from some of the more rudimentary materials, I thought, that had washed ashore. But we don't have enough rations because you've eaten everything, the captain began to explain. Even the cheese and crackers? I inquired doubtfully. Yes, the cheese and crackers were gone too, the captain haplessly acknowledged. We were drinking brandy from giant sifters and laughing and the captain drew on his enormous Cuban cigar, producing a thin puff of smoke. Then he raised his eyebrows and put out his hands to indicate, I thought, how sad it was to end this way. I had just finished an olive loaf. The orangutan was carrying a tire with him and I bit into a salami stick. It's like one of those great Russian stories, I explained. All we need is snow, the captain insisted. So I built a fire and the captain removed his shirt. Then he leaned back in his chair and I noticed the startling tattoo! Are you really a doctor? I said. How did you know? the captain said. You're a chiropractor, aren't you? No, no! he laughed. Of course not! Actually I'm a podiatrist.

My God, if I don't get some sleep soon I'm going to be a complete zombie tomorrow. I'm going to be all spaced out! And don't you think that little bitch won't be looking to sink her fangs into me! Don't you think that little bitch won't be trying to give me the goddamn run-around!

Did I tell you about her? Did I tell you about the goddamn meeting I have with that little bitch tomorrow morning?

Goals! Maureen said. Fucking goals!

What about goals? I yawned.

I should tell that little bitch to shove her goals straight up her goddamn fat ass!

...I mean two weeks ago there was so much yelling over there I thought somebody was getting murdered for Christ's sake! And then last week I figured I'd get up nice and early to go for a run before work to clear my head just like we talked about, and what do I see but some drunk bastard passed out on our front lawn!

I mean is it me, or has this world gone half crazy? I mean is it me, or can you imagine seeing something like that?

...And then they're always racing their goddamn motorcycles up and down the street like it's a goddamn free-for-all or something! Like we live in the middle of some goddamn desert. Or out in the middle of Ohio! Ohio, for Christ's sake! Or goddamn Montana! I mean what the hell would happen if we *had* kids? Or a dog *even?* Have you considered it? *Well, have you?!*

I said, Maureen, why don't you just come back to bed?

Maureen said, I should go over there and burn that goddamn house down!

I reached for the blanket and Maureen forced the window open, and all of a sudden a blast of cold artic air pushed its way through and I shivered!

Please, Maureen, I said. Please, it's cold in here! I started to beg.

What Could We Have Possibly Known About Love Then?

But before I could go any further, she stuck her head straight out through the opened window and screamed: Shut the fucking music off, assholes! Do you hear me?! Shut the goddamn music off! You're not the only ones who live here! You're not the only ones who have rights!

She said, My heart's racing a million miles an hour over this shit! Then: If you think I wasn't nervous before, well, God damn it, I'm sure as hell a nervous wreck now!

I turned over in bed and Maureen started pacing around the room. A little bit of drool had pooled up at the corner of my mouth and I leaned my face into the pillow to wipe it away. Then I yawned aloud. I tried to go back to sleep. But all of a sudden Maureen came over to show me her hands. Which were trembling, or she was making them tremble.

Where are the cigarettes? she said after a while. Where are the goddamn cigarettes?

I brought the blanket up to my neck and yawned. I turned on my side and rubbed my feet together. But someone across the street had laughed and she started rifling through the dresser drawers, mumbling to herself, shifting things around.

They're not there, I said. I sat up momentarily and then I rolled back over and closed my eyes.

We don't have any left?

Honey, why don't you just come back to bed?

Just tell me where they are!

Why don't we just close the window and try to forget about all of this?

No! she said. God damn you! she said.

Listen, it's late, I said. I licked my lips and pulled back the blanket as an offering. C'mon, honey, I said.

The Two of Us Like That, You Know

She said, Are you going to tell me where the cigarettes are, or am I going to have to scream? Don't push me, Jack, she said. Or I'll do it. If you think I'm lying just try me—

I know it sounds silly but the thing with the cigarettes was we were both trying to quit. Of course it had been Maureen's idea. To tell the truth I was hardly a smoker myself, you know, except for the occasional cigarette here and there when we're out socializing with friends or if it happened to be a nice crisp fall afternoon or if it was the middle of the summer, let's say, and I had nothing better to do, et cetera, et cetera.

And so I was fine with it. The arrangement we had—

But then a couple of months ago Maureen came home and said she was giving up cigarettes for good. *We* were giving up cigarettes for good! It was about time, she said. That's it! No questions about it!

She had a plan, she said, and how she'd been smoking since high school and how in retrospect perhaps that had been way too long. And how maybe this was just the push she needed. But she didn't think she could go cold turkey and she didn't want to use the patch. She wanted nothing to do with that disgusting gum. She didn't want to see a therapist either, she said. And for one reason or the other a hypnotist was obviously out of the question. So what are you going to do? I asked her. We were sitting in the kitchen by then, and it was late! And what does this have to do with me? You're going to help, was her reply. You're going to hide the cigarettes. I said, Do you really think this is a good idea? She said, You're going to be the one in charge!

What Could We Have Possibly Known About Love Then?

Maureen slammed the dresser drawer—"I'm fucking losing it! I'm fucking losing it, Jack! I swear to God I am! I'm fucking losing my mind!"—and I crawled out of bed *exhausted!* And I dragged myself down the hall through the family room to the study across the cold tile floor in the mudroom down a short flight of stairs.

In the garage I turned the switch on. I yawned and rubbed my eyes. Then I walked around the front of my car and pushed aside a small garden trowel and some leftover bulbs, a few containers of bird seed and a small rake.

From the bottom of an old terracotta pot I grabbed the soft pack of Marlboros and shook it, stuck my finger through the tiny hole and pushed it from side to side.

Then I took a deep breath and yawned. I stretched and scratched the back of my head and looked across the garage where I noticed the center light in Maureen's car had been left on. And then upon closer inspection that the door had been left wide open with the key in the ignition still turned forward so that the counsel lights were draining the battery too, along with the radio whose volume for some inexplicable reason had been turned down so low that you could barely hear it unless you were sitting inside the car.

God damn it! I said to myself. What now? She'd been in such a goddamn rush when she got home—her temperature was ripe, she kept telling me—that I barely had time to remove my pants before she pulled me into the bedroom and crawled on top of me.

So I opened the car door and sat down. For a moment I looked around the back seat and scuffed my bare soles purposely along the mechanic's paper. (What's good for the goose is good for the gander!) Then I turned the ignition off and then I clicked it back on. I noticed the gas tank had been

126

filled all the way to the brim. Was it too good to be true? Was it a sign? I thought, Does everything in life indeed happen for a reason? I started fooling around with the window regulator for a time. I yawned and scratched my chest. I was only in a t-shirt and underwear still but I went through the center counsel and counted out a dollar seven in loose change. I told myself, I had been in love once, hadn't I? And certainly there was no reason to think I couldn't fall in love again.

And so I leaned back and adjusted the rearview mirror. I turned the radio dial and pushed the button on the cigarette lighter and fifteen seconds later watched it pop. I started thinking: If I left now without looking back, without any hesitation at all, even if I didn't have any particular destination in mind, I could be at least a few hundred miles away from this place by daybreak.

When I went back inside Maureen was sitting on the sofa in the family room. The television was on and she was going through the channels.

I said, Did you know you left the car lights on?

Did I?

You left the keys in the ignition too, I said, and the radio was on.

I put the keys on the table to show her and one at a time she brought her legs to just underneath her. Then she turned back to the television where an elderly man was lying on a couch reading a book, all done up in one of those cotton Snuggies.

She said, I wonder who buys this shit.

I have no idea, I said.

You would never wear one of those things, would you?

I don't think so, I said. Why?

I hope not! she said. God!

She looked at me and pouted her lips and I turned to look outside at the house across the street. I think the party's dying down, I said.

Those kids are really pissing me off! Maureen said.

Maybe tomorrow I'll try to talk with them, I said.

You know if I had a gun I'd probably go over there right now and have a talk with them myself!

I looked at her and she winked at me. Jesus, I said.

Why not? she said. You don't think they'd deserve it. You don't think I'd have standing in the court of public opinion!

She said, You should have seen all the shit I've had to put up with today. Right from the word go!

With work, you mean? I said.

A fucking avalanche of shit. A total onslaught! She said, This has been one hell of a day, brother, let me tell you!

She shook her head and laughed. I sat down and she started flipping through the channels (like she was on crystal meth or something!) and for some reason (I don't know why!) when she came to one of those late-night infomercials for Time-Life Magazine's music collection where a song by Gordon Lightfoot was playing, my mind started to drift back to this one particular long weekend when I was fifteen years old and my family was "vacationing" in Boston and I happened to say something to my father—What did I say? What could I have possibly said?—and he lunged at me (You ungrateful bastard!) and my mother screamed, my sister cried and then I took off, and then he took off after me, and the two of us started racing furiously up and down Faneuil Hall, along portions of the

Freedom Trail, past the giant statue of Samuel Adams with his arms folded, his body fully erect!

How about some coffee? Maureen said after a while.

Do you want me to make coffee? I said.

She said, There's probably no way in hell I'm going to get any goddamn sleep tonight, don't you think? What time is it? What time is it anyways?

It was almost three o'clock in the morning.

God damn it! she said. God damn those fucking bastards!

She looked at me and scowled. Then she started going through the channels again. No wonder this world is half crazy, she said. What kind of person is up at this time in the morning, can you tell me that?

I looked at her and smiled, and then I leaned back in the chair and closed my eyes.

But then Maureen said, If this world is going to pot, then God damn it! she was going to get her kicks too—

Coffee and cigarettes, she said. Then: Smoke 'em if you've got 'em!

But obviously there weren't any cigarettes left to smoke—

…What do you mean they're all gone? How can they be all gone? I thought there were eight cigarettes left. Isn't that what *you* told me last night?

I don't know what you want me to say, I said.

Did you smoke them all? she said. Don't tell me you smoked them all for Christ's sake?

I shrugged my shoulders. I yawned. At first I pretended not to hear her, and then I turned around to look outside.

God damn it! she said. Only me! This could only happen to me! It's like I have a target on my back! Is that it? What a goddamn night this is turning into!

What Could We Have Possibly Known About Love Then?

I went into the kitchen to make us some coffee. I took out the pot and put in the filter, ground the beans and had it all ready to go when Maureen said on second thought she didn't want coffee. Coffee isn't good for you, Jack! I don't think you should have coffee either! How about making us some of that green herbal tea with a little bit of honey and lemon? Doesn't that sound good? Don't you think that would be better?

So I grabbed the teapot from the cabinet, filled it with water and set it on the stovetop with the flame turned on high. Then I picked up the newspaper from the kitchen table, glanced at it quickly, grabbed a pen, and went over to the refrigerator and added to the list of things I planned on doing by the end of the week.

For instance, when I saw Tim Crowley at the liquor store Monday afternoon he said what a surprise it was to hear that Westerfield's had closed. That was a pretty big shop after all, he said. *What were there, a hundred? A hundred and twenty-five of you?* And to think they'd close the doors like that without so much of a warning?

I told him I'd been there for more than eight years. I was a lead man. I said, This is the first time since I've been sixteen years old that I've found myself without work, and I hardly know what to do.

The teapot started hissing and I turned the dial off. I reached into the refrigerator for the lemon and the cupboard for the honey. I kept telling myself it had only been a couple of weeks now, and we'd always been pretty good about keeping a rainy day fund. *Thank God!* And it was only the two of us after all. Besides, when we got talking Tim mentioned something about the new government contract

Remington had signed, and how he figured there'd be a bunch of job openings down the road. I don't think it'll pay much, he said. It's just monkey work really. But if you don't mind getting a little grease on your hands at least it will keep the lights on.

...I just don't get it! Maureen started calling from the other room. I just don't get it one bit!

What's that? I said.

What? Maureen said.

I shut the refrigerator door, peered my head through the opening from the kitchen out to the family room. What don't you get? I said.

People! she said. Goddamn people! Jack, for as much as I want to, I just don't get people!

I brought the tea out and set it on the table. Maureen had spread her work pad on the sofa and was trying to determine her three main goals. Mainly, she said, she wouldn't mind gouging her boss's eyes out when she had the chance. Was that a goal? Or maybe when she wasn't looking she'd poison those disgusting tuna fish sandwiches she brought to work with her every single day.

I told her how I'd already scheduled a meeting with a headhunter for next week, and how I'd planned on giving Tim Crowley a call first thing in the morning. I said, Maybe I *am* a bit overqualified for that job, *like Tim said,* but you have to admit it's a good company after all and if I got my foot in the door and established myself, well, you never know, stranger things have happened.

Amen, brother! Maureen replied. A-men! Isn't that the truth! she said. From your lips to God's ears! No, I don't think truer words have been spoken!

She said, You should have seen all the crap that was getting shoveled my way! You should have seen the attitude that little hussy was giving me!

With work, you mean?

And what did I do? she said. What did I do to deserve something like that?

I sat down and grabbed the remote control. I was flipping through the channels hoping to find a movie. Like Sergio Leone's *Once Upon a Time in America,* which I had seen the week before. But there was nothing on, nothing worth watching anyways.

And then I came upon that *Seinfeld* episode with Babu, the one where Kramer had stolen a jacket and Elaine was taking the IQ test for George.

Naturally I laughed out loud. I was noticeably exhausted, but I couldn't help it!

But then Maureen began mumbling something about the car, something about Gus and the car and that little hussy he'd been seeing. And so I turned away from the television at once and I watched Maureen squeeze the lemon and mix everything with the spoon.

All week long, you understand, ever since Maureen came back from visiting her sister and the kids two towns over and told me about the rattling noise she'd heard coming from underneath the hood, I had been worried about the car. To tell the truth I had been on pins and needles. I had been worried about the car and Maureen and me, and how much all of this was going to set us back.

The Two of Us Like That, You Know

So I said something about it. I said, What's the damage? Give it to me straight! What happened, Maureen? What did he say? And don't you dare sugarcoat it whatever you do!

I turned back to the television and outside someone screamed. I put down the remote control and Maureen raised the cup to her lips and blew.

Then she started laughing. For some strange reason she started doing this thing with her hands!

...And all at once I had that feeling of some old-time worn-out broken-down boxer, blood spraying everywhere as the knees buckle, the stomach turns over, and he pushes on forward toward the center of the ring.

I want the truth, I said. Tell me the truth. God damn it, Maureen. Stop fooling around.

You want the truth? she said. Do you *really* want to know what happened?

You heard me! I said.

Excuse me?! she said.

For God's sake, Maureen! I said.

"......"
"......"
"......"
"......"

...Well then, fasten your seatbelts! Because this is really going to throw you for a ride!

...And so I brought the car in like I always do, like I've done for practically the last ten years of my life, you know, nothing's changed in that regard. And naturally I see Gus right out front, and *naturally* when he sees me he comes right over and the two of us start talking. I say, Gus, I have a problem, and then I pop the lever to lift the hood and go to get out of the car. But as soon as I start telling him about the noise I heard the other day when I was driving back on Route 25, he looks me up and down and says, What's wrong? What's wrong, Maureen? Tell me! he says. I've known you long enough to know. What's wrong? I say. There's nothing wrong, I say. And he goes to lift the hood and I look at him and smile. But he keeps pressing. I'm all ears, he tells me. He says, Use me as a sounding board. If I can't tell him, then what? Maureen, he says, that's what friends are for, aren't they? And he puts his hands on my shoulders and again he looks me up and down. Come on, Maureen, he says. Come on, honey. Tell me, Maureen. Let it all out. So I tell him about work. I start there. I tell him about our new neighbors from across the street and how I haven't been able to sleep at night. I say, Gus, I've quit smoking and I show him my hands. But he knows me too well, and when I go to pull away from him he doesn't let me. I say, Gus, I'm all right. Really, everything's fine. But he says, I'm not going anywhere until you tell me. How's Jack getting along these days? he says. *Is he excited?* I've got all the time in the world. So what else can I do?

…And before you know it out of nowhere that little bitch comes running out! You know the one he met in Vermont after he broke up with Janet. That bitch! The one who, for some reason, everyone says kind of looks like me except to be honest I don't see it at all. *Do you remember?* Do you remember I even showed you the picture and you said, Who's that? and I said, Supposedly, it's me, and you said, What are you talking about? That doesn't look anything like you. Look at the nose, for instance, *you* said, the nose is different, and you don't even have the same color eyes.

The Two of Us Like That, You Know

…Anyway, she comes running out, and by now her mouth is going about a million miles per second, and she's throwing this fit, a goddamn tantrum really, about how I don't have any right to be here, and how Gus is not my property. *But who said anything about Gus being my property?* How that ship has sailed, as she said, and how it's time for me to face facts and to do my best to go forward. What are you talking about? I ask her. I say, Who said anything about me and Gus? I even look at Gus and say it. But in the next breath, she threatens to call the cops. Get the hell out of here! she screams. Get the hell out of here! But I tell her I just don't want to be stranded on the side of the road. Gus, can you just look at my car? I say, Gus, please look at my car, and then I'll go.

…Which is when Gus tells me to hold on. Let me send Hector over, he says. Hector? I say aloud. My God, out of everyone possible, he wants to send Hector over. Hector who bumps into walls on a good day. Hector, who takes his tiny flashlight and barely sticks his head in and says, Everything's A-Okay. There's nothing wrong here. You're as good as gold. Everything's tight as a goddamn buckle.

…And as you can imagine I'm crying like hell. As you can imagine, tears are streaming down my face, and I'm just a big old mess, one big ole goddamn mess because of the conversation we were having anyway. You wouldn't even believe it. You need to go! she keeps yelling at me. All right, I'm leaving, I say. And don't you ever think about coming around here again! Go on! Get going!

I turned away from the television and looked square at Maureen who took a good sip of her tea before setting the cup back down.

What Could We Have Possibly Known About Love Then?

She said, Is it me or are people today goddamn crazy, Jack? Is it me or have people just about lost their minds?

I said, Maureen, you can't be serious! I said, For God's sake, that did not really happen, did it?

She said, That little hussy's got her tentacles wrapped around Gus so tight that he hardly knows whether he's coming or going anymore. I even told Gus, Do you really think it's a good idea to have her working in your office? Gus, do you really think it's a good idea to have her meddling in your affairs?

Maureen kept talking. But to be honest by then I didn't give a shit one way or the other, and I turned back to the television and I leaned back in the chair and rubbed my eyes.

And so what are you going to do? I said.

About what? Maureen said.

About the car? I said. The goddamn car!

What about the car? she said.

The rattling noise, I said. What are *we* going to do about the goddamn rattling noise?

Jesus Christ, Jack, have you been listening to me? Have you been listening to a single goddamn word I've been saying to you? I mean have you? For God's sake what does this have to do with the car? Who said anything about a car? Jack, I haven't slept in six months! Six goddamn months! And suddenly you're concerned about a car? A goddamn car? What about me? What about my life? People all around us are living their lives. How about what I want out of things?

Maureen ran off to the bedroom. *Naturally!* And I sat there awhile just thinking, flipping through the channels and thinking about all sorts of things.

The Two of Us Like That, You Know

I said to myself maybe I didn't know my way around cars like Gus did, but I was an engineer after all, I knew my way around systems, and if Gus couldn't take a look at it, well then, I figured what was a car anyway except for an engine block and a radiator, spark plugs, some hoses, belts, nuts, washers, et cetera, et cetera? And if I could do it, why not save a couple of dollars? It probably wouldn't take me all that long—if there was anything to fix anyway—and for the time being I could give Maureen my car, and then beyond that, well, who knows?

I got up and stretched. I went over to the window, took a deep breath and looked out.

From the light of a solitary street pole I could make out the long thin silhouettes of people cutting across the front lawn out to the street corner and the sounds of car doors opening and closing and engines turning over with half-baked music playing while people milled around not yet decided what to do. It's funny, I thought, how when you get to a certain stage you just start looking at things differently. Things that looked one way for the longest time *naturally* seem to take a turn in the other direction. That's why, I figured, you had to give it to Gus in a way. People change all the time but in many ways he'd never changed. I'd been telling that to Maureen for years…not so much out of warning but because it was true. It's like I told Maureen, That girl Janet didn't mean anything to Gus. And I doubted this new girl did either. But whenever I brought it up, whenever she had a problem with her car and "had" to see him, Maureen would just laugh about the way things were then and how they are now and what has come of the thousand miles in between—

We were only in high school for God's sake, she'd say. We were practically babies. That was almost fifteen years ago now, can you believe it? What could we have possibly known about love then?

Her eyes were beet red when she came back out from the bedroom. She'd been crying of course but none of it, she said, was my fault. It wasn't anyone's fault really. But the truth was she simply never imagined it would be so difficult. Did you? she said. Did you think it would be so hard?

Maureen said some people have dreams to live their lives one way while other people have dreams to live their lives another. She'd always had the same dream, she said. Jack, ever since I was a little girl I've only had one dream.

She came over to where I was standing, next to the window, dug her chin into my shoulders and flung her arms tightly about my neck.

What are your dreams? she asked.

How do you mean? I said.

I mean what do you want to do with your life now that you have a second chance to maybe start all over again?

Oh God, I said, I don't know. I hadn't thought about it, I said, and it was true. My whole life, and where this came from I didn't *exactly* know (maybe my father! maybe his father before that!) but I had always been so mindful of just having a job in the first place that I always thought everything would sort itself out later.

I'm tired, Maureen said. I'm so damn tired that all I want to do is to go to sleep and yet all I keep doing is thinking about all the things I have to do for tomorrow.

But you don't have any troubling sleeping, do you? Jack, you sleep just fine.

The Two of Us Like That, You Know

I yawned and Maureen said I'd been mumbling in my sleep during the night. It was the mumbling that had woken her initially. My mumbling, and then of course afterward the music from across the street kept her good and awake.

Now I know all of your dirty little secrets, Maureen said.

Like what? I said.

Like everything, she said. Everything, you wouldn't even believe—

I caught her reflection in the window and shifted my weight. She let her hands fall from my neck, but I did not turn around.

I hadn't done anything yet, I knew. Yes, there was the Russian literature professor I'd seen here and there at the coffee shop who was on sabbatical, she said, to complete her first novel, and then the young Spanish woman with the six-month work visa I'd met in the grocery line who said how nice it would be to have someone show her around America.

But that was just talk. All of it. With both women nothing had materialized to this point.

So I asked Maureen again. I was curious. I wanted to know. So I said, Like what, Maureen? Maureen, what did I say?

Do you really want to know? Maureen said.

Yes, I said. I really want to know.

Maureen looked at me with a sly, devilish grin and I rubbed my eyes and made stars. Neither one of us saying anything for a time.

And then all of a sudden, Maureen said, The Swede needs food! The Swede needs food! The Swede needs food! The

139

Swede needs food! The Swede needs food! The Swede needs food! The Swede needs food! The Swede needs food!

She started poking me in the back and I turned around at once and took a deep breath afraid I was going to hit her.

The Swede needs food! The Swede needs food! The Swede needs food! The Swede needs food!

I don't understand, I said. I don't know what you're talking about.

The Swede needs food! she said again. The Swede needs food! The Swede needs food! The Swede needs food!

I put my hands up, and Maureen said, All goddamn night all I kept hearing was, The Swede needs food! The Swede needs food! The Swede needs food! The Swede needs food!

Is that right? I said.

I thought I was going to have to hurl myself out the window! Maureen said. Or maybe glue your fucking mouth shut!

God that's strange, I said.

You're telling me.

I wonder what that means.

You really don't know?

I shook my head. But then I remembered how my uncle used to work with this guy everyone called the Swede. But that was such a long time ago, I said, and I hardly knew the guy. So why would I be dreaming of *him* all of a sudden?

I have no idea, Maureen said.

Neither do I, I said.

Maureen said, I wanted to cut your fucking tongue out of your mouth, you know!

She took a giant step forward and gave me a big smile. Then she started poking me with her long fingernails again and I backed up, squeezing my fists.

Anyways, she said, I'm going to get dressed.

Where are you going? I said *thankfully.*

I'm going to run out for a pack of cigarettes, she said. Since you've smoked them all, *you bastard!* Then maybe I'll just drive around for a bit, and get lost myself, you know. Before I have to race home and get right to work. I have so much work to do.

With the goals, you mean? I said.

Goddamn goals! she said. Then (she winked): Fuck that little bitch and the goddamn horse she rode in on!

How about you? she said.

What about me? I said.

What are you going to do? she said.

Oh, I don't know, I said. I'm kind of tired. Maybe I'll just watch some TV, you know.

Maybe you can buy one of those robe blanket things.

Maybe I'll buy you one.

Sure! Maureen said. Can you imagine? Me wearing one of those? And the dog? If we get a dog, that is, he can wear one too.

I said, The guy on TV sure looked comfortable, didn't he?

Why not? Maureen said. That might be a pretty good idea after all. The two of us like that, you know.

There was a noise outside and I turned back toward the window and looked out. For some reason (I don't know why!) I started wondering if kids that age still drank keg beer, and then of course what kind…and how long it had actually been since I got rip-roaring drunk at a good old-fashioned keg party in the woods? I started thinking, Maybe when Maureen left, I'd get dressed and comb my hair and grab a bottle of scotch from the liquor cabinet and go over. I didn't think the kids would mind. I had a decent single malt scotch after all. And certainly they'd have cigarettes. There'd be no doubt about it! And without parents around there was always the possibility of reefer!

Hey, I have an idea! Maureen said.

What is it? I said. But before I could *adjust* she quickly pressed her breasts against me, reached into my shorts and started jerking my cock the way she knew I liked it…over the tip with a good amount of spit!

Are you hungry? she said. Are you hungry?

How do you mean? I moaned.

It's going to be all right, Jack, isn't it? *I moaned again!* Just like you said, Jack, everything's going to work out just as it should.

Afterward she turned around and started down the hall, whistling, licking her fingers, swinging her hips back and forth all the way to the bedroom door as I reached for the cups on the coffee table *limply* and stumbled into the kitchen to put everything away.

From the previous morning a mound of dishes had stacked up in the kitchen sink.

But I'd barely got the water going before Maureen came tearing back down the hall, sliding into the linoleum kitchen (at what seemed like warp speed!) half naked still but now with her little pink and white tennis socks on.

Jack! she screamed. Jack!

I had the teacups in my hands but I was merely holding them by the saucers.

Jack! she screamed again. Jack! Jack, do you know what we should do?

I turned around at once and she gave me that look. What is it? I said. What's wrong? I said. My God! I thought. What now? And my hands started rattling and I could feel I was losing my grip.

I took another deep breath in and Maureen threw her long hair back...as though a reply! Then she took another step forward and all of a sudden I was like a ghost. I could feel the blood draining out of me.

Listen to this, Jack! I mean it! Don't move! Listen to this!

So I crossed my legs at the ankles. Then I looked down at my feet.

What is it? I said again. Maureen, what's wrong?

...Jack, I think we should go straight out to Lenny's and buy an entire carton of cigarettes. I'm talking a whole boat load. The whole kit and caboodle. And whatever strikes your fancy too. I don't care. Whether it's Marlboros or Parliaments, American Spirits or Camels, Mores, Lucky Strikes, Newports, Benson & Hedges, what have you. I mean we'll smoke every single one of those goddamn cigarettes right down to the filter, all the way through! I say we go for it, Jack. No rules. Let the past be the past. All that. No holds barred.

...And then when we can hardly breathe anymore, we'll go to that Greek diner on the Post Road and order a king's feast! I'm talking pancakes with syrup, bacon and eggs, hash browns and sausage, French fries drenched with chili and cheese, that disgusting key lime pie you're always talking about! You name it! We'll eat and eat and eat and eat! Hell! And if you want to get drunk, we can do that too, why not? And then when we're good and ready, when we've had our fill and we can hardly stomach another bite, I'll call that little bitch at work and tell her I've suddenly come down with the flu, and we'll race back home together and crawl right back into bed and press our bodies up against each other just like we've been doing lately and then try and then try again.

And Besides, That Was a Long Time to Be Best Friends with Somebody

…What are you, Ann Landers?

Who?

Ann Landers, I said.

I'm serious, he said.

I know. That's the problem, I said.

You just have to trust me. You're going to be all right. You're going to be just fine, you'll see.

Do you really think so?

I know so, he said.

I don't know, I said, shaking my head. I wish I had your confidence.

Sure, he said. You just have to give it time, that's all. Maybe you can't see it now, of course, I get it. But in a little while you'll hit rock bottom and then everything's going to be all right, everything will be smooth sailing from that point on—

Oh, I don't know, I said.

Sure, he said.

Because she took everything, you know. *Everything,* except for the dog.

What Could We Have Possibly Known About Love Then?

Well, at least you have the dog. Look at it that way. You love that dog, don't you?

Not to mention the half dozen vacations she took with *friends* the last year and a half we were married. Don't forget about that. I told you about that, didn't I?

…Besides as far as I see it she did you a favor.

Is that what you'd call it?

Sure, he said. Why not? Think about it! he said.

Oh, not this again, I said.

…Because once you hit the bottom you'll have nowhere to go but up. Once you hit the bottom you won't sweat any of the small things, and you won't ever look at life the same way again.

It was one of those early summer days in July, sun-splashed, and with a good amount of heat and down by the shore the kids were running back and forth between games of tag and Marco Polo and "mud balls" and Denny laughed to himself, then leaned his head back and took a good swallow of beer, stood and then carefully scanned the beach up and down.

So how's work going? I said to him after a while.

It's all right.

And your brother? I said. How's your brother?

He's all right, I guess.

What's he been up to?

Dougie? he said

No, Dave, I said.

Who?

Dave, I said.

Oh God, he laughed. I have no idea. To tell you the truth I was going to ask you the same thing.

I looked at him. What do you mean? I said.

I never see him anymore.

How is that possible?

I never see him, he laughed again. Then he took a good swallow of beer and called down to his son.

I said, But don't you work with each other every day? Aren't your desks in the same office?

I started laughing.

Please, he waved his hand. (He had been doing that all afternoon!)

Have you talked to him?

Not for a while, I said.

You see?

He looked at me and then he looked back at the shore. I laughed and he leaned his head back and drank more beer.

He doesn't return any of my phone calls, I added.

The dude's a wreck.

How so?

He's just fucked up, that's all.

You mean because of her? I said.

He waved his hand.

And *how* many months pregnant are *they?* I said, and he waved his hand again.

I said, My parents ran into him the other day at *Dominick's,* and they said he looked terrific. They said he seemed pretty happy too. In fact, my mother couldn't stop talking about it.

Talking about what? he said.

You know, how good-looking your brother is, how well-mannered he is, so on and so forth…

It's all a façade, you know.

What do you mean? I said.

Did she mention the glasses?

What Could We Have Possibly Known About Love Then?

What glasses?
He said, You think you've got problems!
What's this about glasses? I said.
The dude's losing his mind.

He drained the rest of his beer and asked me to reach him
another and I opened the cooler and the beers were ice cold
and I handed him a beer and grabbed one for myself and told
him how it all kind of reminded me of those trips we used to
take together when we were *much* younger. Like to Montauk,
I was thinking. Or the Berkshires. Or when a bunch of us
went to Woodstock, Vermont that time. Not to mention all
those lost summers we had in Newport, Rhode Island when we
were still in our early twenties and we'd just hop in our cars
after work late on a Friday night and drive two hours north
along 95 whether we had a place to stay that weekend or not—
I said to him, Remember that trip we took to Syracuse to
visit your buddies Mike and Tony from college?
Remember that? he said. Now *that* was some trip.
Not really, I laughed.
I drained my beer and cracked the other beer open.
Sure, he laughed, you were so drunk and there were all
these girls…
We were all pretty drunk if I remember. Even Dave was
drunk—
…And then at four o'clock in the morning while everyone
else was dancing around the bonfire there you were pounding
your fists in the sand over your ex-girlfriend.
I looked at him and smiled. C'mon, I said.
Am I lying? he said.
I don't remember.

That Was a Long Time to Be Best Friends with Somebody

You *don't* remember?

I was out of my mind.

Oh, you were out of your fucking mind, all right. He laughed. Then he shook his head. Then he leaned his head back and had a good amount of beer.

I blame it on the whip-its, you know.

He waved his hand.

And the mushrooms didn't help any.

He waved his hand again.

Neither did the nitrous bombs.

…And it was one of the most beautiful nights ever and Neil Young was playing and all night long out in the middle of this giant cornfield as far as the eye could see all these incredible long-haired hippie girls in sundresses and Birkenstocks kept coming out of virtually nowhere—

Those were the days, I said.

Do you remember that? he said.

I think Dave fucked one of those girls, didn't he?

…And there you were pounding your fists in the sand.

C'mon, I said.

It's not true? he said.

Well, I shrugged my shoulders, I loved her. I thought she was the one.

Jesus! he waved his hand.

And if I remember correctly even *you* thought she was a *terrific* girl!

She was all right, he said.

Just all right?

She was all right, he said again. (But then I noticed the corners of his eyes were smiling!)

So I asked him what he meant by that.

Then I said to him, You wouldn't lie to me, would you?

What Could We Have Possibly Known About Love Then?

About what *now?* he seemed to laugh nervously.

About sleeping with her? I said.

What are you talking about? he said.

I said, You know *exactly* what I'm talking about.

Oh God, he laughed, and then he waved his hand. And then he turned right back around and stood, took a few steps forward as one of the *other* boys screamed.

I said, Do you remember that time we went to your cousin's party and I got so drunk that somehow or the other I ended up pissing on that guy's Jeep, and then before you knew it, while you and Dave and Dougie and Vinny Discenzo were playing beer pong and having one hell of a good time, well, that one guy had already pinned my arms behind my back while the other guy—who Mindy, your cousin, later said was a middleweight Golden Gloves boxing champion from the city—literally beat the living hell out of me?

What made you think of that? he said.

Well, do you remember? I said.

2.

We'd been drinking for several hours already and when I walked into the kitchen Tina was standing there in her *sheer* black bathing suit with her back toward me and her hair done back in a long ponytail putting together some turkey sandwiches for the kids, and as I stumbled over to one of the countertop stools and started looking around the place I began to wonder what would happen if I simply walked up to her and pulled down my shorts and did some sort of a reach around and started fondling her breasts.

What's fair is fair, right? Do unto others as only you would have them do unto you?

…So, how's everything going out there? Tina said.

It's all right, I said.

And how's he doing? she said.

I think he's tired of watching the kids, I said.

He's tired? she laughed.

They *do* have a lot of energy, I said.

Don't I know it, she said. I'm their mother after all.

She looked at me and smiled. Then she grabbed the jar of mayonnaise—it was one of those Hellman's squeeze bottles. And for a moment I wondered if perhaps she was the type of woman who liked to play games. Not like Udo Berger and El Quemado in *The Third Reich*. But games like *Cops and Robbers* or *Naughty Nurse*. *You've been sent to the principal's office!* And what about: *FTA Agent versus Muslim Terrorist?*

It was always possible, I thought. Though we'd known each other quite a long time and certainly in public at least she didn't exhibit any interest in that type of behavior.

But who could tell really? Who knows what happens to people behind closed doors? And you can't tell me that sex doesn't do strange things to people…

I said, When we were kids we used to spend our summers at Lantern's Point but those were just shacks really. They weren't anything like this. I said, This is a hell of a place. It's nice around here.

Isn't it? she said.

It sure is, I said.

She said, We tried to get the same place we had last summer, you know, but the people ended up selling it over the winter.

Is that right?

Now *that* was a *nice* place, she said. Do you remember? Over there just beyond the reef.

She pointed, and for a moment I followed her long creamy fingertips…to her breasts, and again there were those thoughts but I simply shook my head no.

You don't?

No, I said.

She put both hands on her hips and I spun around on the stool.

I never went, I said. Don't *you* remember? We'd just come back from St. Croix—the *Virgin* Islands, I laughed. It was supposed be a vacation, of course. But that's when I almost killed her. And then a week later the lawyer suggested I move out of the house.

C'mon, she said.

Don't you remember?

That was last summer already?

Can you believe it?

She looked at me and laughed and I lifted my beer and drank it. And out of nowhere, it seemed, although this happens from time to time, I must admit, a shiver of tumult (rage and lust!) ran down my spine. "Do it!" I could hear her say. "I'm going to fucking kill you!" was my reply. "Do it!" I could hear her say again. "I don't think you have the balls!"

Tina picked up the knife. I looked at her and winked. What? she said. What are you thinking about? But then I spun around on the stool and she buttered the sandwiches and cut them in half.

Then she went over to the refrigerator and grabbed a head of lettuce, two tomatoes, a large cucumber, an avocado, and a red and a yellow pepper.

Do like feta cheese? she said.

152

That's fine.
How about pumpkin seeds?
All right.
Craisins?
She came back over to the counter and put everything down. Then she arched her back some and moaned, removed the yellow elastic from her long brown hair, and ran her hands *suggestively?*
I feel like I'm falling apart, she said.
Since when?
Do you really want to know?
I took a good swallow of beer and nodded my head and Tina moved her neck from side to side.
And then *inexplicably* she reached her hands high above her head (as though she were preparing for a cliff dive).
And when was the last time you talked with her? she said.
In February.
And she lives in New York *now?*
Manhattan *supposedly.*
But she works in Bridgewater still?
That's what I'm told.
And *how long* does it take for her to get to work in the morning?
Almost two hours, I think.
Each way?
I nodded my head and Tina cut the lettuce into cubes, grabbed the colander and went over to the sink and turned the faucet on.
…And she has a roommate named Michele, I said.
A roommate?
And apparently Michele is a Calvin Klein model.
Is that so?

What Could We Have Possibly Known About Love Then?

And apparently Michele plays guitar and *he* writes poetry, and *he* competes in no less than a dozen marathons each year along with *his* volunteer work for the lost children of Peru—

Wait, Tina said.

For what? I said.

But her eyes suddenly widened, and before she could turn away she was already laughing.

I'm sorry, she said.

No, go on, I said.

I didn't mean anything by it.

It's only my life.

She shook out the colander and grabbed one of the big ceramic salad bowls.

On the countertop there was a stack of brochures and I grabbed the one with the giant manatee on the cover.

Of course she was laughing still, and to be honest it was getting slightly *irritating!* And so I said to her, Did you know the greatest threat to the West Indian manatee population is the potential future loss of warm water habitat? Not to mention vessel strikes "which have been determined to be the greatest limiting factor to the speed at which..."

...And it's not like we didn't try to warn you, she said. It's not like *he* didn't try to say something to you after all. But what could he say? What could anyone say? She waved her hand at me (just like her husband, I noted—that bastard!) and rolled her eyes. You were, she started laughing again! *In love!*

Bullshit!

You don't think so?

I don't remember him saying anything.

Oh yes.

When? I said.

Plenty of times, she said. Trust me. I was there. And c'mon, did you ever *really* love her in the first place? Because I never saw it to tell you the truth. None of us did. And don't you think it's time to be honest with yourself?

I looked at her and shrugged my shoulders. Well, she smiled. *Well,* and I drained the rest of my beer and went back to the brochure again.

In the meantime she had picked up the large cucumber and had said something rather *lewd* about Michele!

Basic Facts Regarding the Florida Manatee, I read aloud.

You see? she said.

"The Florida manatee is a large aquatic relative of the elephant. Sometimes referred to as the sea cow, *these slow, lumbering underwater creatures have thick, wrinkled skin on which there is often a growth of algae..."*

Tina said, Have you ever seen a manatee before? In real life, I mean?

No. Have you? I said.

Once, she nodded her head, a long time ago, when I was just a little kid, and I was probably only seven or eight years old at the time—

Around Dennis Jr.'s age, you mean?

That's right, she said. And we were visiting my grandparents in Fort Myers. And my grandfather—God, rest his soul!—used to have this tiny wooden boat, this tiny crawler we'd take out. My father, my brothers and me. Sometimes my grandparents too. But my mother never went. Because she couldn't swim. Even to this day. Isn't that ridiculous? All these years later...?

I said, It says here that the average adult manatee is about ten feet long and weighs between 800 and 1,200 pounds.

They're big, Tina said, very big. But very stealth-like too.

What Could We Have Possibly Known About Love Then?

She diced up the cucumber and laughed. I shook my head and she moved her neck from side to side. Then she scooped up everything and started to mix it all together in the bowl with the two large wooden spoons.

I still remember, she said. We were going around this inlet. This tiny narrow inlet that led out to the bay. And it was one of those bright picturesque afternoons, you know. Just like today, in fact. Sun-splashed. And there wasn't a cloud in the sky. And everything was bright and completely calm all around, and we were just sailing along in this tiny boat as though we were in one of those biblical stories, I guess.

Is that right?

When all of a sudden there was this incredible rush of water. What the hell is that? I thought, you know. My God, I didn't know what the hell it was! And then the boat started to rock back and forth. And I started to look from one side of me to the other. And for a split second, I swear, I remember thinking I was pretty sure that I was going to get tossed overboard. And then maybe it was my brother Mark, or *rather,* maybe it was my older brother Jerry, or maybe even both, I don't remember, but whoever it was started to scream, Shark! Shark!

Shark? I said.

Shark! they screamed. And then they started waving their arms wildly about!

But I didn't think the manatee had fins, and I told her so.

They didn't of course, she said. And of course they were only trying to scare me. They were only trying make me cry...

I said to her, Did you know the name *manati* comes from the Taìno, a pre-Columbian people of the Caribbean, meaning "breast"?

That Was a Long Time to Be Best Friends with Somebody

…And relatively they're extremely gentle creatures, she said. But of course when you're not expecting something like that, one way or the other, it catches you off guard.

Tina started to set the table. I offered to help, but she told me to relax. You've been through enough, she said, and how I was *their* guest after all.

And so I put down the brochure and started to walk around the place, where on the first floor it was one of those big wide open spaces with beautiful hardwoods and big comfortable white beach couches with blue pillows and those decorative rattan chairs with plenty of windows all around.

It must have cost him a pretty penny, I thought. Probably somewhere in the ballpark of seventy-five hundred dollars a month, or maybe even ten thousand, given the location—

But why not? I said to myself. *Even then.* It wasn't like he didn't work hard for it after all. And just because you happen to be down on your luck today, well, that doesn't mean you have to be in the same place tomorrow.

Tina poured herself some wine. Do you want any wine? she said.

No, that's okay, I said.

Are you sure? she said.

I nodded my head and then I walked over to the cupboard and searched around for the bottle of scotch.

What are you drinking? she said.

Scotch, I said. Do you want any?

I grabbed the bottle of scotch and showed her the blue label.

No, that's all right, she said, and she showed me the great big glass of wine she poured.

C'mon, I said. Why not live a little?

What Could We Have Possibly Known About Love Then?

I grabbed a small rocks glass off the counter and went over to the freezer for some ice.

She said, Did he tell you we're going to Florida?

When? I said.

In September, she said.

I looked at her and then I opened the freezer door. So he didn't tell you, she said. No, I said. Why doesn't that surprise me? she said. And I shut the freezer door and walked back over and grabbed the bottle of scotch.

So who's going? I said.

Everyone, she said.

The kids you mean.

And Dianne too.

Oh, Mrs. Green is going? I said to her.

Because we're going to Fort Lauderdale, she said.

Fort Lauderdale? I said.

And Dianne is going to watch the kids for a couple of days.

It was the annual sales convention for the network marketing company Tina had been working for—the one that for months now she was trying to get me to buy into. *Cosmetics? Anti-aging formulas, health drinks and the like?* Because, as she said during one of the vehicle presentations in May, both Denny and I thought you'd be perfect for it. You're smart and good-looking and you've been around business all your life. Plus, it'll be a good way for you to meet women, don't you think? Not to mention the fact that it was, of course, a ground-floor opportunity, and how brick and mortar stores were, as I probably knew, a thing of the past, and how pretty soon, in a few years, you'll see, all businesses will be operating this way…

Besides, everything's paid for, she said.   Food, drink, entertainment, the rooms. She showed me the brochure of the *Riviera Hotel,* which was a five-star hotel in Palm Springs.

The only thing we have to pay for is the flight!

And you're going to Fort Lauderdale? I said to her.

Yes, afterward, but only for a couple of days.

And he didn't say anything to you?

About the trip you mean?

About his sister? she said.

His sister? I said.

Lainey.

What about Lainey?

That's the reason we're going to Fort Lauderdale in the first place.

She said, For the longest time he wouldn't talk about it, you know. He wouldn't even mention her name. But over the last couple of months, ever since I booked the plane tickets, he's been talking about it more and more. Not that he's told me everything, of course, and not that I dare ask. I know him well enough to know that, she said. And yet after all these years I still don't know what really happened to her, except from what I've been able to glean from a handful of old newspapers, some old articles that I found through the university...

But even then, she said, there are large gaps. Timeframes. Things missing. Bits and pieces unaccounted for.

She said, All I know is that she was talking with someone earlier in the night. An older guy maybe. Maybe around our age *now*. You know, around thirty-five to forty years old. But then all the girls left the bar together around one. And then they all went back to the hotel together. And yet when her friends woke up the next morning she was gone. And when the police went to investigate her room there wasn't anything to indicate foul play. Nothing at all that looked suspicious. Nothing, for example, that indicated forced entry.

…So when he started talking about it the other night, I just kind of casually asked him afterward, Did she leave a note? Did anyone call her room? Did they see anyone go up? Was there any noise? How about the hotel cameras? Did anyone at the front desk see her leave?

And what did he say? I said.

Well, you know Denny, she said. He didn't.

He doesn't know, you mean?

He didn't say, she said, and to tell you the truth the only one who's ever really talked to me about her is Dave. Dave's been the only one really.

Not Dougie? I said.

I figured if anyone would have talked to her about it, it would have been Dougie.

No, she said. Not even Dick and Dianne. But it was Dave who told me all about it when we first started dating. He was the one who told me when I first saw her picture at the top of the stairs.

Do you know that picture? she said.

I did.

She was very beautiful, wasn't she?

Yes, I said.

And what else?

What do you mean?

What do you remember?

About his sister? I said.

About anything, she said. About anything at all.

The phone started ringing.

That Was a Long Time to Be Best Friends with Somebody

Because you've known him as long as anyone. In fact, you probably know him better than me—

She said, For some reason he doesn't remember that part of his life, you know. And you can understand it, she said. I can't *even* imagine. It must have been an awful time.

I grabbed my rocks glass and brought it to just underneath my lips.

And she'd just graduated from high school, she said.

We were all so young.

It must have been terrible.

We were only eleven years old at the time.

3.

"Did you see that?"

"Did I see what?"

"You mean you didn't see that?"

"What are you talking about?"

Denny swallowed his beer and stood, and then he put his hand to just above his eyes and carefully scanned the beach.

Over by the concession stand, I noted, Dennis Jr. and the two other boys were running wildly back and forth still while down along the shore Denny's daughter and her friend were building a sandcastle with a large mote all around.

She's easy, Denny said, turning around quickly to look at me. You don't have to tell her anything twice, nothing, nothing at all. Not to do her homework or to get ready for bed at night or to brush her teeth in the morning, or anything like that! But with him, he laughed—and then he looked over at his son and started waving his hands again, calling to him—

everything's one big pain in the ass, a complete shit show, a nightmare to tell you the truth, you wouldn't even believe it!

He said, This kid's going to turn me into a complete alcoholic, you know!

And I looked at him and laughed, and I told him, of course, that I didn't think he needed any help there.

A few minutes later Tina came running out.

What took you so long? Denny asked. What the hell were the two of you doing in there anyways?

And then afterward when the three of them were safely inside, Denny looked at me and winked and he pointed across the beach just beyond the lifeguard stand in the direction of that young woman in the yellow bikini with the long brown hair (who just a half hour earlier he had insisted was at least twenty-three years old, and maybe she was, while I had this sudden and overwhelming feeling that just as easily she could have been as young as sixteen).

…And there you were pounding your fists in the sand, he laughed. While you had it all, everything right there, everything a person could ever want right there in front of you.

Well, I loved her, I played along. And is that so terrible? I said.

Then: You have to admit it yourself. Love can make you do some pretty strange things.

He looked at me a moment, and for a long time I wondered what he could have possibly been thinking. But as though he could read my mind he started to wave his hand again as he proceeded to tell me about some kid two houses down, who was a real pothead, he said, and how just that morning he'd bought a pack of *Marlboros* at the liquor store which he'd hid inside his car's glove compartment for later, for as soon as Tina had gone off to bed.

I said to him: You can't tell me that Tina doesn't know you still smoke cigarettes from time to time—God no, he laughed—and how even though he had this whole operation down pat, I'd witnessed it hundreds of times over the years, to be honest I found it all rather impossible to believe!

Then I said to him, Do you remember when we used to go fishing at Lantern's Point and you'd keep the packs of cigarettes under that old *Gators* hat you wore to make sure they didn't get wet?

C'mon, he laughed.

What do you mean? I said.

We had known each other almost thirty years, ever since we went to grade school together, and in all that time we'd never talked about his sister once (not that I wasn't open to it but I think we just felt there were some things between us better left understood). Like when I told him I was going to try my hand at writing and he asked me what I was planning to write about—

And besides, that was a long time to be best friends with somebody.

driving along
north adams road
in god's country, connecticut

where my grandfather
spent
nearly half his life
planting flowers

you'd never think
the economy was
in the fucking toilet,

unemployment
at an all time high
and people
losing their homes

at a record clip—
until you considered
the reason(s) for it:

the need
for losers
for benefactors

(to the victors go the spoils)

and men
red hot

under the sun

with shovels and rakes in hand

alongside machinery
churning and burning,
mixing and pouring
water rock and sand

for foundations
for mansions
they'd build—even bigger

Chapter 1

I was happy to find myself alone that summer day standing there in the old R.L. Sullivan wing of the preparatory school I attended on Great Barrington Road wherein the faces of those hall of fame men attached side by side in photographs lined upon a beige wall I at once saw myself on some lazy spring afternoon wildly anxiously unknowingly in row amongst the others fresh-faced young men like me but not like me anymore leaning back in hard wooden chairs and pushing our luck for all it was worth against this great balancing act we hardly understood.

Perspective

There were photographs all over the house. Black and white photographs, old Polaroids. Grainy colored pictures on the walls and on the end tables, on the refrigerator and the window sills. There were photographs of Jenny and me from when we were first dating and photographs of the two of us years later when we were first married and living on the third floor of that old apartment on Wade Street above Carl and Dale Nelson and old Mrs. Winters.

On the mantel there were photographs of Jenny growing up out in the middle of Ohio and photographs from those years she was living in New York City and attending Parsons College and going through what she called her *alternative* phase.

In a way it was funny seeing the photographs like that, all lined up and side by side.

In this one photograph, in particular, Jenny is standing in the middle of a giant field during what looks to be late spring or early summer and everything is green and bright all around and she is wearing a sundress and her hair is long and there are two boys laughing off to one side and the wind is blowing lightly against the trees lifting the branches and there are white puffy clouds scattered here and there and it seems as though at any moment there might be a little bit of rain and then the sun and then a giant rainbow stretching all the way across the Heavens…

In another, Jenny is sitting in a dark pub in Greenwich Village and she is nineteen and her boyfriend Steve is twenty and they are both dressed in black and they are both wearing black eye shadow and Jenny's hair is dyed green and pink and cropped in one of those pixie cuts and Steve's hair is equally strange and they both have dour looks to their faces and one arm around the other and maybe Jenny was happy, this is true, and Steve is giving someone or the other the middle finger—

Most of the photographs I'd seen before but some of them looked new to me and were difficult to place.

When the phone rang I had been looking at this one photograph of my father and me and my son from when my son was no more than six or seven years old and we were all sitting in the same living room that I was standing in today.

In the photograph my father is sitting to my son's left and I am sitting to his right. I was wearing a mustache then and my father had on these thick glasses and my son's hair was long (as his mother liked to keep it) and coming out of his ball cap, and he was smiling and my father had his hand on my son's shoulder and the three of us were looking straight ahead.

What we were looking at I don't know. Probably Jenny. Or more than likely my mother. In any case I narrowed in on my father's hands. When I was a boy he carried around with him these strong cement-like hands. Exacting hands. My father was a carpenter by trade but mostly he bore a mason's resemblance.

You can always tell a lot about a man from the handshake he gives, my father taught me early on. If it was too strong, he'd say that was one thing. Too soft, well, that was something else entirely. A man *always* needed to be judicious, he *always* needed to find his own way in this crazy sentimental world. Nothing is at last sacred but the integrity of your mind. Regardless the way the wind blows, Raymond, above all a man needed to be self-reliant...!

You want to laugh—

There was this one birthday party we had for my grandfather when he was living at the convalescent home and had just turned eighty-four years old (eighty-four years young, as he was telling everyone that night) and I went to grab our coats to leave and my son went to kiss my father good-bye.

Naturally, my son was just a baby then, and mostly what had happened was that Jenny was holding him too loose and my son simply squirmed away (as boys are wont to do) and leaned in too close. Anyways, my father pulled back immediately. *You should have seen the expression on his face!* Then he looked at my son...and then he just glared back at me. I was handing out coats at the time and didn't know what to say, of course. But to be fair we'd just come back from the *Great Rivers,* where Jenny's family did a lot of hugging and kissing was encouraged.

So where were we? Jenny said. What were we talking about? What's next? What are we going to do now?

You were telling me about your conversation with Larry, I said to her.

Oh that, Jenny said.

She walked down the hall from the study, and I picked up one of the lamps to show her.

What Could We Have Possibly Known About Love Then?

Larry was one of the lead engineers at the Thomaston Environmental Agency. Jenny had worked with him for years. His name was Lawrence Oliver Bennet III, and he wasn't all that bad. People called him Larry for short.

Jenny nodded her head. Then she returned the phone to its cradle, took a step back and looked around the room.

So what happened? I said to her.

This doesn't bore you? she said.

No, I said. Why would it?

I looked at her thin lips and her painted fingernails. At the white t-shirt she was wearing, right around the breastplate.

Oh, I don't know, Jenny shook her head. I'm not *even* sure it's all that important. I'm not *even* sure it really matters anymore, you know. I mean in the grand scheme of things, *Who are we? Who's going to listen to us?* Maybe it's like Larry said. Why kick over a hornet's nest if you don't have to? *We're just a small organization after all.*

But that didn't sound like Jenny, and I told her so. And for that matter it didn't sound like Larry either.

And for some reason, I don't know why, I was suddenly reminded of something my Uncle Sal used to say about the rubber and the road, and the thick of the stew, and how everything else is just wishful thinking—

Jenny looked at me and smiled. Then she tilted her head slightly, and bit the bottom of her lip.

So what would *you* do? What would *you* do if you were *me?*

Oh God, I laughed.

Then, regarding the old lamp, she said, Over there. Let's just put it over there for now.

Perspective

The phone started to ring again—it had been ringing off the hook ever since I got there *early* that Saturday morning; who the hell was calling? I thought; I didn't recall the phone ever ringing that much when I lived there!—and Jenny leaned over the old sofa and stretched. Then she moved her neck from side to side.

And then, *I noted,* she took her long slender fingers over the old fabric, tracing its design.

I think we should go out the front door with this one, Jenny looked up at me. I think we can do it in one shot too, don't you think?

If that's what you want, I said. It's all right with me. You just need to let me know, I told her. If it's too much, you just need to give me the signal.

Oh, I'll be all right, Jenny laughed. You don't have to worry about me.

You just tell me, I repeated.

Just worry about yourself.

We walked around the sofa and positioned ourselves on opposite sides.

Off to the right on the bottom of the frame I could feel a nail head poking through, and so I dropped to my knees and slid my hands over to try and get a better grip.

How's it going over there?

It's all right.

Are you sure? Jenny said.

I'm okay.

...Because I'm ready whenever *you* are.

I looked across the sofa and straightened my back. Thick strands of long blonde hair fell across Jenny's face and she blew at it, and I solidly planted my feet beneath me.

You just give me the signal, I said.

What Could We Have Possibly Known About Love Then?

Are you ready? she said.

You just let me know.

On the count of three, all right?

She looked at me and blinked, and I slid my hands over again and tightened my grip.

Are you ready? she said.

I'm ready, I said.

Okay then. One...Two...*Threeee!*

We'd spent most of the morning clearing out the family room, going through *our* things, keeping some and making a pile of the rest. The old Flanagan's furniture, and such (which might not mean anything to anyone today, but you should have seen the look on Jenny's face all those years ago when that bright red Flanagan's truck first pulled into the drive and the two men with the white gloves and the spotless red and white Flanagan uniforms stepped out...I swear, you would have thought we'd hit the lottery!). And by the late afternoon we'd taken the last of the old furniture down to the curb to make room for the new furniture that was being delivered on Monday. The night before Jenny had made a few signs. Free furniture, one read. Years of happy memories, another. And as she leaned over and began placing the signs, I stood there looking at her all over again wondering if maybe that was her way of trying to tell me something after all, if maybe, like my mother had said, we did have a chance to make hay out of all this mess I'd created.

When she'd called me a couple of days ago, after she had called the rest of *our* family and friends to see if anyone might be interested in the old furniture, she said she'd thought about taking an ad out in the paper but a *friend* didn't think that was

172

such a good idea. She said a *friend* had told her about the time he'd taken an ad to sell an old car, and all the crazy people that had come out. *So* why not just get a dumpster and load it all in there, her *friend* had said to her, and be through with it? Or call one of those junk removal services and make it easy on yourself?

Apparently this *friend* had another *friend* who did that sort of thing for a living, Jenny said, and *apparently* that *friend* owed him a favor. *So* it wouldn't be a problem. It was no problem at all. Just to let him know and he would take care of everything. Once and for all she could wash her hands of the whole damned business.

But Jenny didn't think it was that simple. For one reason or the other, she said, she'd come too far to begin making hasty decisions now. Besides, the way she saw it, she said, there was still some life left in those old sofas and end tables, the television stand and chairs, and *certainly* there were plenty of people who could have used it these days. *Certainly,* with the economy the way it was, there was someone out there who could see the value in those things.

I put my hands on either side of my hips and arched my back trying to work the kinks out. God knows I was in some of the worst shape of my life. Even Jenny had expressed some concern. Of course I denied it. But God only knows even a blind man could have seen what a wreck I'd become.

So I bent over to tie my laces and Jenny started arranging the furniture by the curb. She moved one piece a few inches forward and then that same piece a few inches back again like she was vacuuming the dining room or the study. I wanted to laugh. I wanted to say, *What do you think you're doing?* But just a few minutes earlier I caught myself doing the same sort of thing. I caught myself looking down at my hands.

What Could We Have Possibly Known About Love Then?

I don't know what you'd call that type of behavior.

I spent the next couple of hours driving around. I went to the video store and then I went to the Seven-Eleven. I drove to the mall and then to the old Dugout to see if my buddy Teddy Moynihan was around, and then I bought a pack of cigarettes and then I drove down to the beach.

At the coffee shop on the corner of the Old Post and Mill Plain Road I was hoping to run into this short blonde I'd met a couple of nights earlier who was an assistant editor of a high fashion magazine, she said, and rather smart and young and quite good-looking with these bright green eyes and this tight little body to her and nice boobs, though she had a husband she loved *very much,* she told me, and a couple of kids herself.

But when I pulled into the parking lot it was mostly empty, and when I went inside to look around the older man with the two suitcases was there and he was already in the process of laying everything out on the table. Which I didn't need to see, of course, not then anyways. Besides, if you stayed too long, that is if you stayed right up until closing (when the staff started to go around with the mop and the bucket and the small dust broom), well, eventually he'd shut himself in the bathroom awhile, and regardless where you sat, even if you put yourself on the other side of the room, it didn't matter, the water would be going the whole time, and he'd be flushing the toilet, and he was always mumbling something to himself anyways or hacking up a bit of phlegm or blowing his nose or humming some old ballad from the three or four records he carried around with him.

It was hard, hard I tell you. Those days driving around without any particular destination. Going from here to there, from one place to another. Never knowing what to do next. Just killing time.

From outside the house on Old Battery Road the lights in the family room looked off, and for a moment I just stood there in the driveway looking at the bright stars against the dark sky, at the outline of the tall trees all along the property…

The video store didn't have much—it was just a small local cooperative—but I picked up a couple of videos anyways. But when I opened the door, the small reading lamp in the family room was on—I was surprised—and my mother, who pretended not to see me at first, was lying there on the couch in her white robe and red slippers.

You're up late, I said to her.

Oh, hey Ray, my mother said. How are you, *honey?* I didn't even hear you come in. Did you just get in? How was your night? How did everything go? Did you eat already? Did you and Jenny have a good time?

She looked at me and smiled. What did you get, *honey?* Anything good?

And I walked around the room as she swung her body forward, assuming an upright position.

What are you reading? I said to her.

You know, I don't even know, she said. *The witches of something or the other.*

I put the videos on the coffee table. Then I picked up the paper, and she turned the book over and edged her glasses down a few centimeters to see.

It was *The Witches of the Country Road.*

Have you heard of it? she said.

I hadn't.

Well, she nodded her head. It was Margaret's turn to choose. She rolled her eyes.

You don't like it? I said.

Well, you know Margaret, my mother said. You know how she can get.

Right, I said. Although the truth was I hardly knew the woman at all.

What time is it?

It's late.

My God, does that say ten o'clock? Could it possibly be ten o'clock already?

My mother squinted her eyes. Then she started to push herself up.

Dad's in bed? I glanced at her.

About an hour already. She grabbed a Kleenex from her robe pocket and blew her nose.

Are you hungry? she said.

I'm all right, I said.

Well, how about some tea? *Honey,* can I make you some tea?

I don't want you to go to all that trouble, I said.

What trouble? she said. It's no trouble.

There's nothing to it, *honey,* she said. *Honey,* it's only water.

I knew she didn't want to talk about it, I knew my mother well enough to know that. But as I was going through the paper—as I was reading through the headlines, scanning through the photographs in the *Sports* section—it was really beginning to tear at me, it was really beginning to make me think.

I knew my father had an appointment that morning at St. Mary's Hospital with Dr. Melenick and Dr. Cavalieri. But, of course, it was late, I could hear my mother say, and how she was noticeably tired, *exhausted* really! I haven't been able to sleep a wink all week, have you, *honey?* You wouldn't even believe it! *Do you know how difficult it is to sell real estate these days?*

She filled the teapot with water and turned one of the burners on. Then she opened the refrigerator and started to take the food out.

Chicken and potatoes, a small dish of artichoke hearts, some homemade bread, a small salad.

So how's Jenny? my mother said after a while. Did you tell Jenny we say *hello?* Did you tell Jenny we send our love? I like Jenny, my mother said. I always have, and I always will. She said, I have a good feeling about all of this, you know. I think everything's going to work out just fine, you'll see.

Maybe, I said.

I know it, she said.

We'll see, I said.

The power of positive thinking, she said.

Of course the thing with my father's eyes wasn't anything new. He'd had his fair share of problems on and off the past thirty years, so there'd been this history, and certain things were just understood. Like how sometimes (much to my amazement, I must admit it) he simply wasn't capable of making out what was so clearly right there in front of his face the whole time, and how that didn't make him stupid, it just meant he couldn't see. Or the fact that he probably shouldn't drive at night or even on a somewhat cloudy day, as Dr.

Cavalieri had recommended more than thirty years ago. But if he wanted to drive, he was going to drive, and that was the end of it. And if we didn't like it, well too goddamn bad! We could simply get out of the car and find our own way home!

The first retina detached when he was only twenty-seven, and the second one let go just a few months before his thirtieth birthday. Right after he'd quit from Rawley, right after he'd opened his *own* business and we'd moved into the new house, and my sister was just born, and there were all these bills piling up, my mother said, and she was scared, of course, and I was only three or four at the time and honestly I don't remember much from those years anyways...

But then my father knocked a glass straight down to the floor, and a week before that it had been a vase. I had no idea, and then all of a sudden I started to notice all these chips in the plates, all these nicks in the furniture. Not to mention that one day last week when I was getting ready for a hot date (with this young little *philly* I'd met online recently) and I overheard my mother talking to my aunt on the phone. But what's going to happen to us? I heard her say. What's going to happen to him? Ray's been taking care of everything all these years? Who's going to take care of me if he goes blind?

Could he actually go blind?

My mother went upstairs for the night, and I sat in the family room reading the *Witches of the Country Road* for a time. Don't ask me why. Getting up every now and then for something to drink or something else to eat. Like those chocolate cookies my mother started to buy, the ones from The Pantry, the ones she knew I liked...with the chocolate

178

sprinkles on top and the fudge and the melted chocolate square in the center.

I did that for a little while. And then around midnight I went back to the kitchen to grab myself a beer. The latest *Boden* catalog had come with that day's mail, and I looked at it, and then I went over to refrigerator again, then I went to the study, I went outside to have a cigarette and to listen to some loud music, and then I came back to the family room and turned the television on, and then I turned it off, I turned it on again, and then I turned it off again, trying not to think about anything, nothing at all, but then more and more thinking about all sorts of things, random things too, things I hadn't thought about in years, things I'd thought I'd pushed aside or nearly forgotten, but in the grand scheme of things, I guess, things that had been with me all along.

Like that one afternoon I came home from school early—someone had called in a bomb threat—and I found my mother crying at the kitchen table all alone. Or a few years later even when my father walked into one of the local banks and the man with the handkerchief over his face (who was slightly bald, my father said, with big ears) jammed a shotgun barrel against his forehead and told him to get on the fucking ground. Of course my father was living on Capitol Avenue then…with a new *friend*—suddenly he had this whole new group of *friends*, this whole gang, people I'd never heard of before, people I'd never met. And, of course, I didn't see him much then, none of us did, but I remembered asking him months later after he'd grown out his mustache again, after he'd cut that long ridiculous hair, after he'd come to some sort of reckoning, he said, and left that woman and tried to square things away with my mom, right before I grabbed him by the throat, and threw him into the cabinets with everything I had, and threatened to kill him anyways...

What I really wanted to know is what happens to a man when his entire world is thrown upside down. When another man he's never met before jams the barrel of a shotgun against his right temple, or threatens to kick the shit out of him anyways. Does it give you pause? Does your life flash before your eyes? All of a sudden, Dad, do you see things clearly? One way or the other, does it offer you any sort of perspective?

And yet when I met my mother at the Galaxy Diner for lunch a few days after I'd lost my job at the Ryan Griffin Company and then that whole thing between Jenny and me blew up, well, it was my mother who days later said, Don't thank me. Thank your *father*. Not me. Because it was your *father* who suggested it. Your *father* who insisted right from the very beginning that you know this house was always open to you. That you know you always have a place to go. That regardless what's happened in the past, regardless what happens from here on out, that you were his *son* after all, God damn it! And he wasn't just going to sit by idle and watch you suffer.

...And that's the thing, isn't it? That's the whole goddamn thing right there, all wrapped up in a nice shiny package for you! Like what Billy Kenney said in his first novel (between those two characters who meet on a train) about how a man can go his whole life trying to please his father, and then the bastard dies and the son's left behind the podium staring at all the admiring faces alone—

Perspective

I went out to the kitchen and grabbed the rest of the cookies. It was a little after one, but I was hardly tired, so I opened the refrigerator and grabbed another can of beer.

On the television there was a movie I liked, nothing spectacular, but an old black and white I remembered watching with my grandfather once a long time ago, my father's father—God rest his soul! One of those old Westerns where at first there were two men talking, and then another man, and then some unknown woman walked into the room…

I could hear someone coughing upstairs. The sounds of someone gagging, and all that phlegm. It was awful. And I took the *Boden* catalog, and I undid my buckle. Then I turned up the volume and I laid my head against the sofa cushion and drank my beer.

The actress who was playing the damsel in distress was pretty good-looking, very good-looking, in fact. I knew in all likelihood she was probably dead, but at the time she had this thick mass of black hair, these long creamy legs and voluptuous breasts, and I undid my zipper and I pulled my pants down a little and closed my eyes.

Going back and forth between the television and the catalog, I sat like that for a while. It was a long time sitting like that.

With my eyes closed I could hear the sounds of glass breaking, gunfire, a child screaming, and tables and chairs getting thrown about, and I tried to imagine what was going to happen next, what would indeed happen to those two men, and then the other man, and then that unknown woman who walked into the room…!

At one point my leg started to cramp. Undoubtedly, from all that hard work Jenny and I did that morning right through the afternoon. But I refused to move. I refused to give in.

What Could We Have Possibly Known About Love Then?

I had it once, I told myself, and maybe with a little bit of *luck* this time indeed I could have it all, I could have it all over again…!

I thought about all those beautiful photographs, about all those great women from the past.

My heart started racing. *Ah,* I groaned. *Ahh! Ahhh!*

I held that pose as long as I could, and I did not open my eyes once.

"It was some sort of strange dream. Or more like a nightmare than a dream. The type of dream one has from time to time without a clear beginning or ending like being washed ashore finally after several years stranded at sea."

H.T. Woods, 1956

Before Charley, There Was Julie and Dad

I turn on my high beams and then I turn them off. I sit in the car with the motor running and I watch him go with his food and the television and his can of beer.

I know he can see me. He's got thick glasses but his eyes still work, so nothing has to be said in that regard. Besides, he's not one for sympathy, never has been and never will be, and I'm not going anywhere, not now anyways.

It's true that when I first started driving I kept telling myself how in some small way I was going to maybe leave it all behind me, start leaving everything else up to chance.

What do people say all of the time: You do the same things over and over again, and yet you expect a different result, how could you?

So why not go to Florida, I started thinking. Set up shop, buy a small boat there. Maybe hire a few men...!

Is that so unimaginable after all?

...But looking back at that period of my life now, with everything that's happened since, (with perhaps everything that'd been with me all along!) I'm pretty sure I knew where I was going the whole time.

It's early December, you understand, and Julie wants to know what we're doing for Christmas. In a way it's nothing more than that.

What Could We Have Possibly Known About Love Then?

Either we're having Christmas, or she's going to St. Louis *alone!* And then who's going to be the one to tell Charley, who's going to be the one to break his heart?

Christmas is canceled! Santa Claus is dead! So on and so forth!

Say all you want about Julie, and there's plenty to be said where that's concerned, trust me when I tell you! But the one thing she'd never be confused for is shy—

"I'm right here! I'm right fucking here! I know you can see me, so don't you even dare think about it!"

Out of everyone in the neighborhood the Wassermans are probably my parents' closest friends. *Jews!* But this time it's Mr. Costello who asks, Is everything all right? Irene, he says, is everything okay?

Oh, everything's fine, Tom. Everything's as good as can be expected. It's just Jerry, that's all, my mother shakes her head and laughs. I needed something at the market, and don't you know how these horns can get stuck in cold weather?

It's the first snow of the season *naturally,* and my mother's got her white robe on, along with her thick socks and white slippers. And as she races up to the car and catches her breath, I reach for the pack of cigarettes and go to look straight ahead at the neighborhood lights and the Johnston's dog going back and forth with Mr. Costello standing in the middle of his driveway and the Wassermans out there on their front porch.

Are we still on for bridge tomorrow night? Jody Wasserman says.

Sounds like a plan, my mother says.

And tell Don I've got my eye on him, Bill Wasserman says.

Oh, Bill, my mother laughs, you're going to have to tell him yourself.

I take out a cigarette and light it, and then I look over at Mr. Costello and wave. He's standing less than ten feet away, so what choice do I have, what's the alternative?

But ever since I was a little kid I've always had this strange feeling he never did like me. And maybe he had good reason too, maybe there was something there all right. (But *let's face it* in high school I wasn't the *only* one caught climbing through his daughter's window at night—Just ask Bill, I wanted to say; Bill Wasserman was the town's gynecologist, and a *noted* pervert! And the fact of the matter is they didn't call Debra Anne Costello—the Mary Magdalene of the neighborhood, ha!—"Blowjob Debbie" for nothing!)

So I ask her, Has he said anything to you? *Anything?* Anything at all?

But as soon as I start to go there, as soon as I start to tell her what's *really* been on my mind (something I've wanted to say *to her* for a long time now, in fact!), my mother tilts her head *slightly* and winks—*Oh honey, please! Please, honey! It's late. Do you have any idea what time it is?*—and then she looks over at Mr. Costello and waves good-night.

Then she calls out to Bill and Jody Wasserman, and does the same.

She whispers, I wish you wouldn't smoke. You know how I *feel* about smoking, don't you? You know how *bad* it is for you. *You know how it can poke tiny holes in your lungs...*

Are you serious? I say to her. My voice *suddenly* rising!

Oh honey, she shakes her head. No.

And let me tell you something...! I persist.

189

No honey, please, she says. I beg you. Just calm down one minute, will you? Lower your voice! *And let me tell you something first!*

"......"
"......"
"......"

She says, I can slap you, you know that? God damn you, I can slap you right across the face you make me so *mad* sometimes! And don't think I wouldn't do it too! *Don't tempt me!* Don't think I don't have the strength anymore!

These legs may not be the same legs I had in my *early* twenties, she says. I grant you that. But they still draw attention, honey. I still get offers, and don't think I wouldn't try!

She says, What about that time I smacked you so hard it left an imprint on your face for several days? *Have you thought about that?* When was the last time you *actually* thought about that? And how your poor old grandmother threatened to call the Child Services on me. (Go ahead! I screamed. Take him!) And then how I nearly had to call the police on myself to boot, because I was so *afraid* of what *you* were doing to *me,* and I was so *very afraid* of what *I* was going to do to *you* next—

I could've *strangled* you! she says. As God is my witness, I could've *drowned* you! I thought I was going to slit my goddamn wrists! But you were always like that, weren't you? Always going against the grain. Always one for bucking the system. Always poking at me. Poking and prodding at me, like I was a slab of meat, like I was some circus oddity, like I was cattle getting ready for the slaughterhouse. When all I wanted was a little bit of peace and quiet. To read a magazine, or to talk on the phone every now and again. To have friends.

Actual friends! To be able to sit on the toilet and take a crap without getting heckled for Christ's sake!

And what was the point of it all? What was the endgame? Where were we going with all of this, honey? Tell me, because I'd like to know!

…Fourteen hours of non-stop driving to Kiawah Island for what was supposed to be this *beautiful* and *relaxing* "family vacation," remember that? Seven days in *paradise!* the brochure said. Fun in the sun! the brochure said. That beautiful ocean breeze! *What else could a person ask for?* And then all week long while all of the other kids were laughing in their bathing suits, snorkeling, having all this fun by the pool, well, there you were dressed in those heavy black cotton sweatpants and that horrible Yankees jacket. Because you were *bored,* you said. The people were *awful,* you said.

I mean my God, honey, I was getting hives. I thought I was going to have a panic attack just looking at you. Ninety degrees out, and you would have thought it was the middle of winter. *Please, honey,* just take off your jacket! I wanted to scream. Would it kill you to put on a pair of goddamn sandals? And then on top of it…your sister runs off and gets attacked by a swarm of bees. All week long your father is in the infirmary trying to pass a kidney stone. And then out of the blue one night two bats fly through the opened screened window! I should have known then! *God only knows,* I should have known then! (Run for your life, and don't you dare look back!) And there was everyone else from the resort—the mothers and the fathers, the sons and the daughters—all *yucking* it up, and having the most wonderful time.

I mean do you have any idea what it's like to be me, *your mother?* The woman who doted over you, who coddled you, who cheered for you from the stands when you couldn't get a hit…who nursed you when you were sick, *my little baby!* who gave birth to you in the middle of an ice storm, for Christ's sake! Nineteen hours of *hard labor!* Nineteen hours of the most *excruciatingly violent pain of my life!*

And where did it get me in the end? That's what I want to know. What's the big prize here, honey? Except for this *constant* siege and bombardment, this *constant* duress and incoming from all sides…

I mean look at me, honey. I'm all skin and bones here. I'm one of the walking dead. I'm a vampire! I'm growing old right before our very eyes, and I hardly know what to do about it anymore!

Damn you! she says. And damn him too! You should be *fucking* ashamed of yourself! Your *poor* mother! Take a good look!

Tossing and turning every night. Staring up at the ceiling like a goddamn zombie!

It's like I told your father, either you're with me or you're not. Either you become the man I'd fallen in love with all those years ago, or pack your goddamn bags because I'm going to go out and find somebody else.

Like John Ingleman, I tell him. Or Paul Abernathy. You know Paul, don't you? What about Phil Eckert? she says. And don't you dare think for one moment I'm not leaving this hell-hole if this ship doesn't get turned around right now!

I mean I'm not a young woman anymore, honey. And that's part of it, sure. But on the same token let's not fool ourselves here. I have needs too! I have *passions* and *desires!* There's still blood coursing through these veins! For God's sake, I'm not dried up yet. I'm a human being after all!

She says, Did I tell you that Maria quit? That's right, she just up and left. That bitch! That skinny little good-for-nothing bitch! Not even two weeks' notice or anything. Just out the door. Gone. *Sayonara! Hasta la vista, baby!* But I guess that's what you get for treating some *illegal* just like family. Smiling at them. Doting over them. Asking them all of those frivolous little questions about their homeland. And for what? That's what I'd like to know! So they can stab you right in the back? So they can drive the stake right *fucking* through the first chance they get? Talk about gratitude! Because if she can get an extra fifty dollars a week, well then, why shouldn't she? If suddenly my ninety-six-year-old father falls down and breaks his neck tomorrow (after risking his life all those years scaling some of the tallest buildings in this country, riveting all those steel I-beams together), well, what skin is it off her nose? She has a right to make a living too, doesn't she? Isn't that the reason she crossed the border *illegally* in the first place?

Isn't that the American way after all?

…And then to have to listen to your aunt drone on and on *endlessly* about it. Your aunt, my sister, the *queen bee,* who nobody's *even* heard from in the last six months! What are we going to do with *him?* she says. *Him!* And how we better put our heads together, and do it quick. Because *obviously* he can't live by himself. But *obviously* he *can't* live with *them* either. *Nick* won't allow it, she says. *Nick!* And besides, they're all going to St. Bart's for the winter (her, Nick, Ed, Dianne, Cathy, Frank, Bill, Susan, Tom, Lisa, et cetera, et cetera)—because she's tired, she says; but tired from what? I want to know—and the house is already paid for, so what choice do they have, what else can they do?

So just call Ritchie, she says. *Who?* If you have too much on your plate, call Ritchie and have him take care of it. And I almost had to laugh *out loud* (right there over the phone!)

because if it wasn't for all of your uncle's "great ideas" over the years, all of those "extremely *lucrative* business ventures" he'd had with those bums from the club, well then, maybe your grandfather wouldn't have been in the hole for all that money, and then maybe, just maybe, that skinny little good-for-nothing bitch would never have left in the first place!

Ha! my mother says. Ha, ha! It's like I have a target on my back. This enormous bullseye. I'm telling you, if it's not one thing, then it's another.

And everybody's afraid, she says. *Have you watched the news lately?* Everybody's got one foot dangling right over the edge.

And now *you* want sympathy from *me?* After everything *I've* done? A woman *my* age? Well, I'm sorry, honey. But you can go straight to hell!

She says, Didn't I tell you it wasn't a good idea? Didn't I say that to you right from the very beginning? Get it out of your minds, and do it quick! I said. Whatever you're thinking, I said, it's just *not* that way. You both *know* better than this, *the two of you.* You have your whole lives ahead of you still, and nothing could be further from the truth. So what did you think was going to happen?

That all of a sudden everything would change? That all of a sudden things would get that much easier? Not to mention all that money we'd spent over the years on private schools and colleges. All of that money, and then all of that time. And not only for you. But for you *and* your sister. The two of you together. Do you know how many sacrifices we made?

Not that I regret it, honey. Not that I wouldn't do it all over again if I could. That's not what I'm talking about here, that's not the point at all. Were you the easiest of children? *God no!* Could it have been a whole lot worse…?

194

Before Charley, There Was Julie and Dad

But then for you to get this *idea* in your head (and where it came from I still don't know!) that maybe it would be good for the two of you to join forces, to get in the trenches, as they say, to work together side by side, well, I'm sorry, honey, but I just didn't buy it. I didn't buy it then, and I *certainly* don't buy it now no matter how many times you try to explain it to me.

You can't reinvent the wheel, you know. You can't turn back Mother Time. And we can stand here talking about it until we're blue in the face, but that doesn't mean we're going to be able to change anything.

Up every morning at four-thirty, not coming home until nearly seven o'clock at night. And what did you think was *really* going to happen crawling around in that dirt all day, working alongside *those* people, riding around in an old rusty pick-up truck...while everybody else's son, everyone else I know, for God's sake, who don't have half the smarts that you do—never did and never will, honey! and I don't give a damn!—are walking around in expensive three-piece Italian suits, sitting in nice cozy temperature-controlled offices with four weeks paid vacation a year and sick days up the wazoo. And there you are up to your knees in the muck—I don't even want to think about it!—swinging a hammer, climbing those old rusty ladders, breaking your goddamn back, running around as fast as you can just to keep out of the cold!

And sometimes I think it's me! Sometimes I say to myself, Where did I go wrong? Wasn't I a good mother? What did I do to deserve these things?

Think about it, she says. Think about Charley, and then put yourself in my shoes.

I mean do you have any idea how sick and tired I am of having to hear about Rachel's kids? Or Jan's? How *they're* doing! What about the Fiteleson girl? I've told you about her, haven't I? How she's working with that famous director *now*. How she's going to all these fancy premiers. Dinners at Nobu! How she's hobnobbing with one *celebrity* after another!

And who the hell is she? I mean it, honey! What kind of stories has she ever written? What awards has she ever won? What kind of grades did she ever get in school?

Did she have art lessons and music lessons and batting coaches when she was young? Considering the fact that we came from *virtually* nothing, honey—your father and me *both* growing up in "The Hollow" as poor and desperate as we did, *have you thought about that one?*—what have any of these *other* people ever done with their lives?

I mean just the thought of your sister working in that filthy community center day in and day out, surrounded by all those goddamn nutcases, well, let me tell you something, honey, it's just about enough to drive any mother crazy. Not to mention the fact that she has her master's degree. Her master's, for God's sake! And then that loser goes off and kills himself, and then all of a sudden it's your sister who comes under fire, your sister who's supposed to turn around and look herself in the mirror and come to some sort of fresh understanding?

Well, I'm sorry. But no, I don't apologize one bit. I thought I'd heard it all before, that's true. But then you just come to a certain point in the road where it's just not right anymore. It's just not right, honey!

Your sister says she wants to live a simple kind of life, but what kind of life is so simple when that old Volkswagen van breaks down again not even a couple of hours on their way to Maine, and your daughter calls in a state of panic and says, What now? It's Sunday. Nobody's open. What are we going to do? Is Dad there? I can't talk to you! Is Dad there? Please put Dad on the phone!

Before Charley, There Was Julie and Dad

...And to think *she* can't talk to *me?* Have I missed something here, honey? You know your sister better than I do! God forbid I open my mouth when she's around—

My mother shakes her head and laughs. And then she looks up at me and smiles.

She fusses with her robe as I draw on the end of my cigarette and French inhale! and the Costello's light blinks on again and Mr. Costello opens his front door and sticks his head out.

But of course this time there is no reason!

You tell me, my mother says. Because I'm all out of answers. I'm tired. I'm worn out. I tried my best—*that* I can tell you! Your father and I, we were young and we were very much in love. But maybe I didn't know what I was doing. Maybe I *was* a lousy mother after all.

She looks at me, and then she tosses her hands. She yawns and stretches her arms as tall as possible and I turn my head to say something when all of a sudden a car full of loud happy teenagers roars down the street and the Johnston's dog comes tearing around the corner and I grip my hand around the steering wheel and then I catch myself.

The snow is falling steadier now. And I smoke my cigarette right down to the filter, and I watch the flakes go one at a time, and then I close my eyes *momentarily* and I see them crashing down on us all at once.

I'm forty-two years old, I started thinking. *How the fuck did that happen?* And in another month I'll be forty-three.

What Could We Have Possibly Known About Love Then?

Oh honey, my mother says, and I turn the high beams on, and then I turn them off.

Oh honey, my mother says again. Don't you think it's time to get out of the cold?

Melissa, that time nearly twenty years ago now when I was skateboarding in the neighborhood trying my best to show off I'm sure you don't remember but I do that simple wave of your hand as you stood at the end of your driveway in torn cutoff jeans and a white t-shirt going through a stack of mail with the wind blowing back your long brown hair.

We are never truly without. Nor left completely alone. Life is not haphazard that way. It cannot be thusly bought and sold. There is no life in extremes, she told me once. No promise in the particular season. For even a mighty drought carries with it some great intention. As does the devastating flood, and what we'd called happiness then. We learn that silence is given a measurable tone so that we may draw comparisons. The way a child gazes at his own reflection, for instance. Or an adult moving in and out of memory. The glint of light through morning shades and what comes afterward. The loss as much as what is gained.

For more than a year now (when it was too noisy to remain at home) she would come by the café and visit. He'd be well into his work by then. But would hear the sounds her shoes made against the hard wooden floor, and call to her. She would pretend not to see him at first. Then come over immediately afterward and take hold of his hand. That year she always had a new hairstyle, it seemed, or was planning a trip to Europe, and eventually he would ask about her husband and children knowing she didn't want to but feeling obligated. She was also thinking about going back to school, she said, and sometimes she would cry as he'd place his arms around her insisting she was a wonderful mother. Usually around four o'clock her husband would call and they'd walk out to her car together making sure nobody was watching. They had been together years before and had loved each other intensely! Most days when the writing was too difficult to bear, they'd go and sit in the small park downtown for hours with their coffees and the chocolate croissant (just like in the old days, she said): watching the young couples drift in and out lazily, talking about the grand stories they planned on writing someday.

Her Recommending Hitchens
from the Maryann Notebooks
Flanagan Wallace

Equidistant to Center

I SEE MY GRANDFATHER SPARINGLY the final year of his life. I see him at Thanksgiving and at Christmas dinner. I see him on his final birthday and I see him the day he dies. The rest of the year I am tied with school mostly.

I am at the marina when my father tells me to hurry home late in the afternoon on a Tuesday as I stand atop a length of floating dock with the sun washing against it reflecting against the metal caps at the pilings and the diminished gloss of the filling station and my legs working against the gentle swells of the bay as a second boat comes in and the arch of the Newport Bridge, massive and elegant, gleams like chrome in the nearby distance.

The day before, I'm told, they have a meeting at the home with one of the doctors who in rotation presides over my grandfather though of course he is not there on the day that he dies.

In a small office in the northernmost wing of the fourth floor of the convalescent home my mother reaches her hand and my father takes it, draws the air from the room and pushes the bad air out as he looks off to his right past the medical diplomas which hang neatly at the wall so that he can turn to face the doctor while tightening the grip of his left hand which traps the blood in place to alleviate the pressure around his heart.

You can hear the fluid every time he speaks, he tells me. It sounds like a drawn out drowning!

Still, I notice, he separates his lips to force his tongue against the roof of his mouth to make words and the nurse takes a damp towel which she pushes into an ice bucket filled with water all the way to the bottom to cool. (But when it comes out of his mouth it is noticeably stained *where it is folded over* and there is too much phlegm to him and he starts to choke right away.)

She is a kind enough woman though, that much is true, and when she smiles he seems entirely happy, and I sit there wondering if she is the Jamaican who gave him a handjob once during the overnight when nobody else was looking.

How does that feel, Jim? How does that feel?

But when she removes the towel from his mouth placing it upon the table *and pulls away!* he draws his mouth shut and looks at her scared, not that he wasn't scared before! as all in all it is not a sound preventative -- and of course there is no cure -- and so his mouth dries up rightly from the air trapped within the drawn curtain while his lips crack deep at the corners and his tongue splits at the top from the back of his mouth to the front and everything forms into open sores and crusts over which is why they use the towel hoping to take it all away.

I arrive on the morning of the day that he dies. His entire mouth is ravaged by then and I sit in a yellow oak chair as they keep it up with the towel anyway; and like a reel of film which I hold up to the light at once he is before me at the edge of a garden bed at the old west property late on a Sunday afternoon in September with the remaining hour of light coming down lifting the flowers from an early morning shower where he stands dressed with boots, a t shirt and coveralls and depresses a wooden handled half moon edging tool into the soil where twenty yards across on a small patch of grass which delineates this bed from a bed of roses there is a small two cycle tiller and next to it a red two and one half gallon container marked ½ gasoline ½ oil.

The teeth of the tiller bare the rich soil of the bed, the shaft choked by stalks of wild bramble; and I watch him depress the blade six to eight inches, kick the bottom of the handle until the soil falls like dense clay.

Twenty feet ahead with the tool, then kneeling at the edge of the bed, I toss a ball high into the air as he shakes out the grass into a white five gallon pail marked California grapes all the way down.

So did you get any hits today? Three. Any home runs? No.

While at the horizon I follow the V shaped trail of a flock of geese calling against the approaching dusk, which, when they have traveled out of sight, leads me to the pitch of the cedar shingle roof from the attic all the way to the gardens at the back where there is a slight wind which pushes the tops of the heathers back and forth like dancing ghosts.

"Everyone from around here has trouble with this C shaped marina," I suddenly recall late at night twenty years later as I'd just come down from the ice house and his body lay still beneath the sheets which stretch entirely from the toes and dip with the legs and rise at the midsection where the stomach is recently distended from the water weight before falling into an inverted arch at the neck.

There are two thin tubes from beneath the sheets secured to the nostrils by a piece of hospital grade scotch tape and I watch my father's sister who I haven't seen in years mashing her hands upon my grandfather's hands in order to get them warm. It is almost ninety degrees in the room and the air is choking from the heat and I look over at my father who looks down into his lap where his fingers are crossed loosely as though in prayer as a rivulet of sweat trickles down the side of his face from the temple and she works their hands continuously as though she is trying to kindle a fire.

You could be such a cold hearted little devil, my aunt interjects as my father looks at her finally and smiles and I sit in this yellow oak chair with thin floral cushion duct taped at the center holding the fabric together and catch the respirator again in between compressions where he is as still as a statue and I cannot recall him being a cold hearted little devil but then again he was not my father.

And of course she was not my daughter, and yet I follow the outline of my aunt's small windswept face from the brow along the ridge of her nose to the chin all the way up to the bag and watch its level. The drip to the bag is slow and there is a deep purple stain which outlines the puncture wound from the needle set to the morphine drip and I make it empty into him so that I can see him dead as I see my grandmother dead the next morning three years earlier, so thin and grey, I stand beside my father who stands beside his father who draws the top blanket slightly to reveal the breastplate as I sit there feeling sick slumped against the back wall of the room mathematically considering the rate of morphine against the time of day trying to distinguish between the heat from the room and the vast amounts of alcohol from the night before as I watch the discoloration in the bag where it beads and begin to process if it has to go all the way through.

"If it does he should have until tomorrow morning." If it doesn't he should be dead by dark!

And I consider consulting with the staff doctors beyond the room to place myself at the small lounge on the other side of the hallway in the corner of the building where the windows run from floor to ceiling creating a panoramic view of the rivers and the mountains behind it and the helicopter manufacturing facility just below...

Which employs half of the citizens in this small town here, one of the beautiful nurses informs me as we sit together and talk and I stare out dreamily at the sun *high in the horizon!* and the momentary interruption of a government issued helicopter which rises exactly from one of three helipads, turns in place, stalls momentarily and cuts through the air above the river until it drops out of sight.

It's the best we can do, she insists. I know, I know. She says, It's only human nature after all. Still it's a damn shame. And I lean against the window and steal away the hands of time where the sun falls beyond the horizon and the moon splits the night's sky in half so that on one side the constellations form and it is completely dark while the rest of it is white washed with the stiff bristles of an old discarded paintbrush.

I have seen that sky once before, I insist, but *only* once...and it is the most beautiful sky you could ever imagine.

So why then must you always leave me—

What Could We Have Possibly Known About Love Then?

From the vase full of flowers my father cut from a hydrangea bush at the west property a few days earlier are pale blue globes, two hands round, but not the deep blue I remembered from growing up when my grandfather added used coffee grounds to the soil.

But they are a wonderful pale blue color, that much is clear, and my father goes from the chair and fusses with the vase. And yet ironically when he pulls the palm of his hand away it is dry.

The invalid next door screams out, I just want to die. Somebody please kill me. I just want to die. I don't want to live like this anymore, and you can hear the rhythmic compression from the two machines as it cycles the air through the clear thin tubes and I continue to study the large wooden crucifix on the wall and my aunt still running her hands along with my father's suddenly lost grey eyes which move ever so slightly when my mother's sick brother labors in to stand against the curtain on the other side which he pushes out with the length of his early stage cancerous body—which smells like smoke, which smells like a toxic waste dump even as he wrings out his hands like he is trying to extricate the cancer from them and my aunt rises out of the seat and wets my grandfather's forehead with a kiss and goes to the small oscillating fan atop one of the end tables by the partition wall to turn it on.

How is it outside, John? she says. Just like yesterday, he informs us all. Beautiful, just beautiful!

And how at times I couldn't understand him. And how many times he now turns around to face me and winks, and rightly ruffles my hair as the air from the oscillating fan pushes and I close my eyes once again with my hands at the back of my head supporting the weight.

I've heard you've fallen in love! he almost seems to shout, and I think how too flawlessly this man is dead.

Who told you that? however I continue to say.

Your mother showed me the pictures. *Ah, Ahh!* And let me tell you she is quite a beautiful girl.

…With the masts rising like newly polished spears, I remember, two and one half stories tall, and the hull perfectly reconditioned, and the stark white underbelly which is newly scraped and painted as it trails beneath the waterline—

The boat swings to the left *almost hitting!* and I reach for the two handed rope where the other boatmen face out from their vessels with large handled brooms…to goad the old captain a bit (just as the beautiful woman in the canary yellow dress and tan boating shoes and the wicker hat which was too big for her face all that summer stands there formidable at the center of the deck still where some moments earlier of course we had laughed together in private, embraced and kissed *because it was supposed to be the last time!*…and when she showed me what she needed to show me, I had confided in her about the other girl).

"Then you should tell her!" I could hear her say. "You should tell her before it's too late!"

…As now I turn to my father who turned to his father who pulled back the sheets to watch that dark Jamaican go down.

The other boatmen sounding off like a group of drunken sailors forever heading into port after six months of rough voyage at sea. The two masted sailboat veers back sharply to the right and we come into the last crawl between the final groups of pilings which settled into a generous bank out to the open waters.

ABOUT THE AUTHOR

J. Wilder-Hall was born in Bridgeport, Connecticut. He is the author of *The History of the World (Love Poems and Other Stories, An American Debut, Vol. 1)* and the short story collection *What Could We Have Possibly Known About Love Then?*

ALSO BY J. WILDER-HALL

The History of the World (Love Poems and Other Stories, An American Debut, Vol. 1)

Having awoken suddenly in the middle of a life without a job, without a home, and with the remnants of a failed marriage all around him, James "Arthur" Blunicki, our beloved wandering poet of The History of the World—aided by a ragtag group of characters, other "strangers" the poet meets along the way—embarks on an epic journey to try to understand everything that has come and gone.

In turns equally heartbreaking and humorous, spiritual and wildly ridiculous, this astonishing debut collection of love poems and other stories reads not only as a visceral roadmap for faith, healing, and redemption, but stands, above everything else, as a collective testament to what is truly possible when we decide to live a life full of hope, love, forgiveness, and grace.